NATIONS APART

A NOVEL
By:
Stephen McGeegan

Order this book online at www.trafford.com
or email orders@trafford.com

Most Trafford titles are also available at major online book retailers.

Printed in the United States of America.

ISBN: 978-1-4269-0820-0 (sc)
ISBN: 978-1-4269-1143-9 (hc)

*Our mission is to efficiently provide the world's finest, most comprehensive book publishing
service, enabling every author to experience success. To find out how to publish your book, your
way, and have it available worldwide, visit us online at www.trafford.com*

Trafford rev. 06/21/2010

 www.trafford.com

North America & international
toll-free: 1 888 232 4444 (USA & Canada)
phone: 250 383 6864 ✦ fax: 812 355 4082

For Silvana,
For her undying love and editorial support

The great themes of Canadian history are as follows:
Keeping the Americans out, keeping the French in and trying to get the
Natives to somehow disappear.

Will Ferguson

PART ONE
NATIONS APART

If you tremble indignation at every injustice then you are a comrade of mine.

Ernesto Ché Guevara

CHAPTER ONE

July 30, 1945
Misión de Nuestra Señora de la Colina
Santiago, Chile

Father Antonio sat quietly in the darkness of his office, taking long, deliberate drags from his Meerschaum pipe. He deeply inhaled the thick smoke from the smouldering tobacco, and then exhaled grey unimaginative clouds. The day after he was ordained, his mentor had taught him that you weren't supposed to actually take the smoke into your lungs, just savour the taste and feel the aroma, let it linger. But he liked the jolt inhaling gave him and it was the last pouch of Oriental Turkish that he had brought from Italy. He intended to get every bit out of it.

The only sound in the room was his breathing, sucking in and blowing out. The grey smoke drifted in the darkness like layered fog, penetrating everything permeable. The long, purple-flowered drapery, heavy enough to block light and absorb the cries of children, stank of Oriental Turkish. He sub-consciously timed his smoking to the beat of the large wooden desk clock ticking towards 8:00 pm. His leather padded chair also let out an occasional squeak, like a kitten's meow, when he shifted his soft, bulky bottom. At forty-two years old, his body suffered from all the effects of inactivity and too much pasta.

With every puff off his pipe, the priest focused more intently on the boy he was about to see. He was not an attractive boy, compared with the other altar servers. He was tall and lanky, his face was scarred from a bad bout with chicken pox, and his eyes were dark and sad. But at thirteen, he was the youngest and the most vulnerable. His parents were middle-class merchants desperate to rise in status, and putting their son forward for the priesthood was one of the rungs on the ladder.

The boy had gone along reluctantly, after his mother had convinced him that he was too unattractive ever to attract any kind of wife. He could do more for the family by becoming a priest. His sister, on the other hand, was very attractive and the angel of the family. She would be able to marry money. She loved her brother and always showed compassion for him. She was devoutly religious, and was the most proud of all of them when he was chosen altar server. Father Antonio thought she would make a good nun, but he knew she would be something more; she was too beautiful and ambitious to be a nun. She would have to remain untouched; it was too late for her.

But it was not too late for her little brother. The boy was ripe. He was a sweet fruit, ready to be picked, devoured and prepared for the priesthood. Soon the altar boy would be a young man, and Antonio would show him the intricacies of smoking a pipe.

He puffed harder, a locomotive steaming towards a train wreck, and began to imagine the young altar server with no clothes on. The boy would have smooth, untouched skin that was crying out to be touched. The priest could feel himself stiffen under the weight of his woollen cassock. He put his pipe down on his desk and turned on the small banker's lamp. The ticking clock showed three minutes to eight. He knew that the boy would not be tardy; he would want to show Father Antonio that he could do exactly as he was told and not discredit his family name.

The priest crossed himself - the Father, the Son, and the Holy Ghost - and smoothed his cassock. There were thirty-three buttons down the front of the black robe, one for each year in the life of Jesus, and he carefully unbuttoned nineteen of them, also a symbolic number, and slid his hand down through the opening.

As the clock ticked its way to eight o'clock, Father Antonio closed his eyes and rhythmically stroked himself in preparation for his nineteenth initiation, his nineteenth virgin at the Santiago boarding school.

CHAPTER TWO

August 10, 1965
Long Lake Indian Reserve
British Columbia, Canada

Peter Frank chose a vantage point on a pine-covered knoll, close enough to watch his children picking blueberries down along the dry creek bed and high enough to survey the surrounding meadows and patches of dense willow bushes. He leaned his 30-30 Winchester against a tree and rolled a cigarette. The smoke would keep the black flies away from his face.

He loved the beginning of fall, especially with a day like this. The leaves were starting to turn colour, the mountaintops were covered with thin lacings of snow and the sky was deep blue. The air had a thin, clean taste.

Now, if the black flies would just fuck-off, he thought and sparked the tip of a wooden match with his fingernail, *then life would be good.*

He had given the kids strict instructions to stay in one place so that he could keep an eye on them. If a bear had the same idea - that it was a good day for berries - Peter would be able to shoot it well before it got too close to the kids. Eleven-year-old Lenny would not have a problem following the simple "Don't wander" instruction, but nine-year-old Christine did not accept boundaries easily. She would surely cross the line, if only because the line was drawn, and Lenny would surely stop her and they would surely fight.

At least, Peter was just far enough away to see everything but, at the same time, not to get involved in the bickering. The boy could settle things without his interference and in the process get a life-lesson in dealing with women. Christine could be a real pain in the ass and whenever Lenny had to set her straight, she would run to him, her Daddy, and play her poor-little-mistreated-girl card. Usually, it worked. Peter did have a soft spot for Christine, even though he knew she was the problem and Lenny was only trying to help take care of her. The boy already had the notion instilled that, because he was male, it was his duty to protect his two sisters.

Rosie was easy to protect. She was the domestic type, not into rough play or challenging herself physically. She cooked and she cleaned, she didn't fight or even argue. She had never posed a problem from the day she was born. She also had an infinite amount of patience with her little sister. Much more patience than Lenny, who was forever frustrated with Christine's blasé attitude that she could do whatever the hell she wanted. And Christine was inevitably blasé with her brother's frustration, which in turn, produced more frustration and usually culminated with foul words and fast feet.

Peter produced a bug-defensive smoke cloud from his cigarette and pondered who would come out best between his little girl and a sow grizzly. He figured that Christine would give the bear hell until Lenny showed up and killed the bear, and then kicked his sister's ass all the way home.

He had just about used up his cigarette when he saw the willow bushes a hundred metres up the dry creek bed begin to move. He narrowed his eyes and saw the black bear's head appear from the camouflage of the bush. With slow, deliberate moves, he dropped the cigarette in the moss and picked up his rifle. He wasn't worried about the children; he was an excellent shooter and the light was good. He could drop the bear with one shot.

As he raised the rifle, he ignored the buzzing cloud of black flies that replaced the cloud of cigarette smoke and focused on the thick layers of fat on a bear at this time of year and envisioned scraping up the rendered fat with salted dry moose meat. He waited for a good shot to present itself. The bear was heading for the blueberry patch, and there was a good clearing he would have to pass through. Peter waited, following the bear with the bead of his gun sight. He could see now that this was a large male. When the bear reached the clearing, Peter sighted in the bead just behind its right ear and pulled the trigger with a steady motion.

The bear dropped instantly, but cried out like a human baby until all its life was exhausted. Peter hated shooting bears for just this reason. Every bear that he had ever shot, he hit with a kill shot and almost every time the bear cried like a baby until its breath was gone. If bear fat wasn't such a necessity of life, he wouldn't even bother to shoot the animal. He didn't really care for the meat. Moose meat was better, and there was much more of it. One moose would keep his family in meat and assorted innards for the entire winter.

By the time Peter had made his way to the dead bear, the kids were there and Christine was trying to cut its throat with the tiny jackknife Peter had given her for her birthday. Lenny was standing behind his younger sister with a sour face and his arms crossed.

"She didn't even know if it was dead," Lenny complained. "She could have been killed."

Peter shook his head. *Kids will be kids*, he thought.

——

Rosie Frank slid the hot pan of chocolate chip cookies from the wood stove oven and replaced it with another. At thirteen years old, she was already more of a homemaker than her mother and did most of the baking. While Rosie loved to clean, organize and bake, her mother dealt with the practicalities of bush life and supplying the basics. In fact, it was difficult to find any similarities between the mother and the daughter. Rosie had her father's tall and slender body, lean arms and wiry legs. Her skin was unblemished and golden; her blue-black hair was twisted neatly into a thick, shiny braid down the middle of her back to her waist. She had her mother's oval brown eyes, but her face took on her father's narrow, angular features.

The aroma of warm chocolate and wood smoke spread through the log cabin and out the open windows over the calm lake and into the surrounding wilderness, alerting the squirrels on the weathered fence railing and the whisky jacks in the surrounding pine trees that cookies were ready. Rosie laid her oven mitts on the table, straightened her cotton dress and admired the first batch. Of course, they were perfect.

Her mother, Sadie Frank, bumped her way through the screen door with an armful of sun-dried laundry and dropped the clothes in a pile on the wooden dining table. She wiped the beads of sweat off her forehead with her bare arm and dipped the blue enamel ladle into the plastic water bucket for a cool drink. She was a small, stout woman, with sturdy legs made strong from carrying pails of water up from the lake, and solid arms that had scraped enough moose hides to make moccasin slippers for every child on the reserve. Her coal-black hair was tied back snugly at the back of her head, giving her round face full exposure. She had a youthful look, despite her brown skin cured by sun, smoke and wind, resembling polished leather. She wore wrinkled cotton pants, wrap-around moose hide moccasins and a Toronto Maple Leafs t-shirt.

"It's nice outside," she said to Rosie in Carrier, her native language. "You should be out there cleaning huckleberries, not in here baking over a hot stove. Save that for night-time, when it's cold."

"I wanted to surprise Daddy when he gets back." Rosie also spoke in Carrier. Her mother's English was minimal, and she used it only to speak with white people, which she did as little as possible. She had never been comfortable in the company of white people and almost never journeyed into town. Rosie's father used English more around the house. He believed the children needed to know both languages. He had spent more time in town dealing with white people and guiding white hunters; he realized that changes were coming to their way of life and that his children would need to be better equipped than he was to deal with the changes. It wouldn't be enough to be a good horse wrangler or hunting guide anymore. The kids would have to be able to read, write and speak English.

Her mother let out a quick cynical laugh. "You mean you want to surprise Lenny and Christine. Your father won't even get the chance to see the cookies."

"The first batch is cooling," Rosie said enticingly. "We better get our share before they get home."

Her mother grinned. "I'll make tea. They won't be home for awhile. They walked to the dry creek for blueberries. And your father was hoping to shoot a bear, so they could be awhile."

"There might not be any cookies left by that time," Rosie speculated.

Her mother took the steaming kettle from the top of the wood stove and poured two cups of hot water, then tossed a tea bag into each cup. "Well, what they don't know won't bother them," she said. "We'll eat your father's share first."

They sat down at the table, sipped tea and munched on cookies like a queen and princess at tea time. They discussed the intricacies of managing woodstove oven temperature and the texture of the cookies they were devouring. Despite their differences, they had no problems communicating and passing time like the best friends they were.

They were well into the second batch of cookies when they heard Christine and Leonard bickering in the distance, making their way down the trail towards the cabin. Rosie stood up and looked out the window.

Her brother walked in front, carrying a rusted metal bucket in one hand, a walking stick in the other and a scowl on his face. Physically, he was the opposite of Rosie. He had his mother's sturdy body and round face, but his father's narrow eyes and coarse charcoal hair. Rosie had seen pictures of Chinese people in old *National Geographic* magazines and, to her, Lenny looked like he was from China.

Christine trailed behind Leonard, talking non-stop, mostly to herself. Her jeans had frayed holes at the knees, and her exposed arms, torso and face were smudged with purple berry juice and dotted with smashed mosquitoes and black flies. The two braids that hung down to her shoulders had little sticks and leaves stuck to them like Velcro.

Rosie's father, oblivious to the children's squabbling, strolled behind with his Winchester 30-30 in one hand and Christine's shirt, shoes and empty bucket in the other. He also carried on his back a pack board weighted down with cut-up quarters of meat. Rosie could see that her father, a tall, skinny man, was hunched over with the weight.

"It looks like father got a bear," she said to her mother as she saw her father drop off the pack board at the meat cache.

"I hope it's a fat one."

Rosie quickly took the fourth and last batch of cookies out of the oven, while her mother went to fold the clothes on the table. "Not bad," Rosie said as she lined up the cookies on the counter. "There's even some left for them."

"They came back too soon," her mother said as she wiped the cookie crumbs from the table. "Another hour and we could have eaten them all."

Suddenly the screen door crashed open and Christine was shoving her way past Leonard to get to the counter. Leonard turned dramatically and swung his half full berry bucket against Christine's forehead with a *bang*. Any other nine-year-old girl would scream and cry after taking a similar hit, but Christine ignored it, elbowed her brother violently in the groin and arrived at the cookies first. She had eaten two before Leonard recovered, grabbed her by the arm and pulled her away.

"We divide them up," Leonard demanded. "Equal shares."

"You can have three each," Rosie's father stated in English as he came into the cabin. He hung his rifle over the door. "And I don't want to hear any arguing."

They sat at the table, and Rosie poured tea for all five of them after putting a plate of warm cookies in the centre.

"Daddy shot a bear!" Christine said excitedly. "A big one!"

"Were you scared?" Rosie asked her.

"She was stupid," Leonard said.

"No, I wasn't," Christine protested. "I cut its throat with my knife."

"She didn't even check to see if it was dead," Leonard continued.

"It didn't matter, I had a knife."

"You are so stupid."

Rosie's father put his hand to his ear. "Somebody's coming," he said.

They all listened and heard the vehicles drive up the dirt road to the cabin and stop. Rosie went to the window and, as the dust cleared, saw a station wagon and a RCMP car park in front of the cabin. As doors opened, a priest emerged from the station wagon and a young, uniformed Mountie from the police car. A cold chill swept over Rosie's body.

"Who is it?" her father asked. They didn't get many visitors.

"I don't know," Rosie replied.

But she did know. This was the priest she had heard about from the other kids. He was taking the children away to some kind of school. Rosie didn't think it would be so bad. She was thirteen and wanted to spread her wings a little. She wanted to learn more English, she wanted to read and she wanted to talk to other kids.

But she knew that neither Lenny nor Christine was going to like the idea. And she was sure that it wasn't going to go easy with her mother.

Her father met the visitors at the door. The priest was even taller than Peter Frank, and he looked down at Peter with stern black eyes. Rosie wasn't sure if he was Indian, although he had brown skin, black hair and a black goatee, but she was sure that he wasn't Carrier. His face was pockmarked and he was much bigger than anyone she knew.

"Good day, Mr. Frank." The priest spoke with a heavy accent as he offered his hand through the doorway. "My name is Father Ricardo." Peter Frank shook the priest's hand a bit reluctantly. "And this is Constable McNee." The young Mountie stood nervously in the background, fiddling with his hat. "May we come in?"

Peter opened the door wide and indicated with his hand for them to enter the cabin. Rosie, Lenny and Christine left their chairs so that the adults could sit around the table. Sadie poured more tea and quickly wiped the cookie crumbs from the table.

The priest and the policeman didn't sit. "We can't stay," the priest said. "We've just come to pick up the children."

"What do you mean, pick up the children?" asked Peter. "Where are they going?"

"To Mary Lake Residential School. You should have received the notice by now."

"We didn't get no notice."

"Do you know how to read, Mr. Frank?"

"No."

"I didn't think so," the priest scoffed. "That's why your children are going to school. They need to be taught civilized ways, to get the ignorant savage taken out of them."

"No!" Rosie's mother yelled out abruptly. "My children stay home!"

"We don't have time to discuss this," the priest said, ignoring her. "The children are coming with me, and the Constable is here to see that it happens within the law."

The young Mountie took an uneasy step forward and bowed slightly. His baby-face expression was serious and anxious, like he knew what was coming next, and didn't like it.

But Rosie had no idea of what was coming next. She had no idea what a priest could do. She had no idea what a church and government would allow.

And she had no idea that it would be the last time she would see her mother and father.

CHAPTER THREE

August 15, 1972
Rawson Prison
Chubut Province, Argentina

Salvador Juárez was well prepared for the mass escape that was to begin at any moment. As he waited in his cell, quietly passing the time, he had meticulously sharpened a steel leg from a bed-frame on the worn cement floor and produced a knife that would make a gaucho proud. He also delicately carved a handgun out of a bar of prison soap that could fool John Dillinger.

Today was the day.

This would be his best chance to get out of this Patagonian hellhole and he was determined to see that it was successful. When he was first thrown into Rawson Prison, he had planned his own escape. But he discovered early on that the political prisoners were well into the initial planning stages of a well-organized mass escape. Salvador didn't give a shit about politics. He wasn't there for his political involvement; he was in prison because he was a paid strong-arm for the man in the adjacent cell, union leader Augustine Tosco. The military government had declared war on any opposition and was systematically murdering, imprisoning and torturing a swath through the union and socialist activists. Salvador had been secretly hired by a childhood friend to watch Tosco's back from the shadows. He had only been on the job for a week when his childhood friend was arrested in a government raid and, after having his penis plugged into 220 volts, gave up several names. One of the names was Salvador Juárez.

Tosco didn't even know Salvador, nor did he know that Salvador had been hired by the union, until they were arrested in the same sweep and dumped in the same prison. When Tosco learned that Salvador was covering his back, he felt somewhat responsible for Salvador's imprisonment. It didn't occur to him that if Salvador had actually done his job, neither of them would be in prison. But then, Salvador was not a professional; he was just a twenty-year-old opportunist. When the mass escape plan began to develop, Tosco decided he would not take part, but he supported the plan and suggested to the guerrilla leaders that Salvador would be a good resource to include in their arsenal. From that point on, Salvador attended every planning meeting and listened carefully. He also did his part in meticulous measuring of every square millimetre of the prison, even though he considered it ridiculous.

All the major guerrilla groups, the Montoneros, ERP and FAR, had underground infrastructure outside the prison and, the way Salvador assessed it, a successful escape depended entirely on outside assistance. To take control of the prison, the planners identified compassion as the weak link in the Rawson security. Most of the guards were simply local hire from nearby Trelew. They could see that almost any of the young men and women languishing in the stark cells could be one of their relatives, perhaps their son or their daughter. The local guards would not put up much resistance. Fazio, a flamboyant womanizing guard, had already been coerced into supplying a FAL rifle and a couple of guard uniforms. Once control of the prison was achieved, a signal would be given to trucks on the outside and the one hundred and sixteen escapees would be transported to the airport on the outskirts of Trelew. Meanwhile, in Comodoro, a couple of *compañeros* would be boarding an Austral commercial flight to Buenos Aires via Trelew. Once the plane was loaded in Trelew and ready to take off, the *compañeros* would seize control of the airliner and hold it on the tarmac until the trucks arrived.

The plan was a little grandiose for Salvador, but he was committed now and was going to go for the ride. He would have liked to fly to Miami, but with the political idealists that he was hooked up with, he knew it would have to be Castro's Cuba or Allende's Chile. It didn't really matter, though; at this point, any country would be a step above Argentina. He just had to get the fuck out of this prison and back on the street.

He had shaved his beard first thing in the morning and tied his long black hair back in a ponytail, which he tucked under his shirt. All the prisoners had let their hair and beards grow so that on this day, when they shaved, donned the guards' uniforms and held guns made of soap and wood, they would not be easily recognized as inmates. Salvador slid the bed-frame knife into his boot and the soap bar pistol into his pocket. He waited for the escape to begin.

—

Esteban Lopez looked in the mirror and a wry grin escaped from his serious expression. He actually looked like a seasoned prison guard, a *yuga*. He was a big man, solid for his forty-four years, and, dressed in the *yuga* uniform, he appeared ominous and dangerous. His thin black moustache made him look older and even more threatening.

But, in truth, he was just a tango dancer who needed a job to make money so that he could romance women and show off his skills at the local tango bar. His sister's boyfriend, Juan, had been a *yuga* at Rawson for two years, and when a job opening came up he recommended Esteban. The prison officials were impressed with both his size and his lack of political ideals, and hired him immediately. Esteban had no intention of doing the job for very long.

But, as it turned out, he loved the job. He didn't really have to do any hard labour and, because he was new on the job, the prisoners he looked after were not very dangerous. Most of them, although twenty years younger than him, had the same kind of family background, listened to the same kind of music, and had the same sense of humour. Esteban couldn't understand why most of them were in prison. But it was a difficult time in Argentina with the military government, it was best to have a low profile and keep your mouth shut. The prisoners he guarded were probably the ones who couldn't do that.

In his heart, Esteban agreed with most of the young socialists and had sympathy for their bleak situation. But he refused to discuss politics, or lack of justice, with anyone. He kept his conversations with inmates short and light. Music was an ongoing topic, from traditional folk to acid rock, Mercedes Sosa to Pink Floyd. A couple of the inmates had pretty good voices, and he was often able to persuade them to sing. Esteban actually looked forward to going to work and being in the company of interesting people from different places.

Clearly it wasn't such a good life for the inmates. Esteban knew there was more going on with them than he was supposed to know, but he played dumb. He had developed a few sources, inmates from the union side, who kept him well informed, as long as he kept them well supplied with cigarettes and *yerba maté*. He knew there was a hole between floors that the men and women used to communicate, he knew there was talk of escape, he even knew about the tunnel they had started digging and had eventually given up. He just didn't care. Their half-hearted schemes kept him entertained and amused. His code of conduct was to keep his eyes open and, except for small talk, his mouth shut.

He wiped the grin from his face, straightened his hat, adjusted his gun belt and walked out the door. Another day of hanging out with interesting people from different places.

———

Salvador was ecstatic.

It started just as it was planned. Fernando, the Montonero leader, showed up wearing the uniform and clutching two FAL rifles. His alert, dark eyes showed no fear, only determination. He opened Salvador's cell and thrust a rifle at him. They didn't need to speak. It was time.

The inner prison went down like dominos. The compliant guards surrendered easily and they were stripped of their shirts and packed into cells. Both floors of men and women had their cell doors unlocked. Political prisoners flooded through the hallways in a kind of organized confusion.

Salvador made his way independently to the door leading to the front gate. He looked across the yard and saw Fernando, Fazio the guard and several of the guerrilla leaders, just leaving to take the gate. A few wore *yuga* uniforms, and they held either real FAL rifles or wooden rifles. Salvador watched the group approach the gate, and he noticed that one young guard at the gate looked confused by the advancing entourage. He said something to his partner, and they both raised their rifles.

Salvador didn't stop to think, he reacted. He quickly aimed his rifle and shot the young guard through the chest.

Since no one saw where the shot came from, both sides shot at each other. When the guerrilla leaders realized that the two guards were down they stopped the shooting and immediately took control of the gates and the armoury.

Salvador lowered his rifle and grinned. Although he had never shot anybody before, he had imagined the scenario many times while watching Tosco's back at rallies. But he experienced an even more powerful rush than he had imagined he would. His hands were wet with sweat and his heart was running on adrenalin. He liked the feeling. He would have liked to shoot more guards, but he wanted even more to be on one of the first trucks leaving for the airport.

——

Esteban was dumbfounded when the escape began; his sources had not informed him. But he quickly recovered. It took only a few seconds for him to recognize that the two clean-shaven men wearing *yuga* uniforms and approaching the first guard with FAL rifles were inmates. He slipped into the electrical room and locked the door as soon as he saw the first guard put up his hands in surrender.

Quickly, Esteban tore off his *yuga* shirt and hat and took off his gun belt. He didn't think any of the inmates would actually shoot anybody, and he was sure that he didn't want to shoot anyone. It wasn't worth it. He stayed in the electrical room with his ear pressed against the door. For a while, there was lots of noise and commotion in the hallway. Then it all seemed to move outside of the inner prison, towards the main gate.

He cracked open the door slightly and looked down the hallway. An inmate stood at the door to the outside with a rifle. His back was towards Esteban, and he was looking across the yard to the front gate. Esteban could see that gate and Juan, his sister's boyfriend, raise his rifle at an approaching group. The inmate at the door suddenly raised his rifle and fired. Juan was pushed back a step when the bullet slammed against his chest, and then he fell heavily to the ground. The group scattered, and more shooting erupted.

Esteban saw the inmate grin after he shot Juan. Enraged, he took his gun from the discarded holster and moved swiftly down the hall to the doorway. He came up to the inmate, from behind, very quickly. In a second he had the inmate's rifle on the floor and his head pulled back by the hair. His gun barrel pressed against the inmate's throat. He recognized Salvador Juárez, even with his beard shaved. He was from the union side and was far too arrogant for Esteban's liking.

Esteban couldn't keep the rage from his voice. "You just shot my sister's boyfriend."

Salvador grimaced in pain. "He was going to fuck things up."

Esteban jerked hard on the handful of hair. "*You* are going to fuck things up!" he growled. "In fact, you've already fucked it up. You shot my sister's boyfriend."

"He was a fucking *yuga*."

Esteban couldn't stop himself. He raised his gun and slammed it as hard as he could against the side of Salvador's head. The prisoner dropped unconscious, the skin on his right temple cut deeply from the steel gun handle, gushed blood immediately.

Esteban pushed the limp body away, snatched up the FAL rifle and disappeared back into the electrical room.

———

Eduardo Garcia could not get past the front door. His ten year old daughter was blocking the way with her hands on her hips, and her large brown eyes narrowed down with determination and strength. She wasn't going to move.

"Please Cosita, I won't be long. I just have—"

"You said that we would go see the whales at Puerto Madryn before they leave." She looked up at him with beseeching eyes, her lower lip quivering.

Eduardo knew she was right. He had promised her. But he had committed himself a week before to pick up a businessman at the Trelew airport, and it was impossible not to be there. He made his living with his car, and even in the small town of Rawson there was lots of competition with the taxis. Eduardo had built up a reputation over the years of being dependable, honest and resourceful. The businessmen in Rawson and Trelew referred Eduardo's taxi to other businessmen. He never missed a pickup and he could always find whatever his clients needed.

But his reputation as the best taxi, and his previous commitments, meant nothing to his headstrong little girl. When she wanted something, she could be stubborn and unmovable. And at this moment she wanted to see the whales in the bay at Puerto Madryn.

"We *will* go," he pleaded with her. "But right now I have a pickup at the airport. I won't be more than an hour."

She eyed him suspiciously, but he could see that she was softening.

"I promise," he added.

Her face suddenly relaxed. "Okay," she conceded, "but don't be more than an hour. We've already lost too much time." She moved away from the door. "I'll pack a lunch so that we won't have to eat at a restaurant."

Eduardo looked at his little girl and suddenly felt sad. She was growing up too fast. It wouldn't be long before she would be gone, living her own life. It was an almost unbearable thought. Ever since her mother, his wife, had died from lung cancer when she was only six years old, the girl had aged years in maturity. She was not just a little girl now; she was his partner and a friend and he was going to miss her when she set out on her own.

He bent down and kissed her on the forehead. "I won't be long."

"I know," she said, with her beautiful crooked grin. "You promised."

———

Salvador had no idea how long he'd been unconscious. His head was bleeding and he found it difficult to think, but he remembered who he was and why he was there. He struggled to his feet and looked towards the main gate. Everyone was still there. He staggered across the yard, trying to stay focused on the gate. His head throbbed with pain and his vision was blurred, but he made his way to where all the inmates were gathered.

Confusion swirled around the group. There was supposed to be a car, and three trucks at the gate. There was supposed to be a signal to let the drivers know that the prison had been taken, but something had gone wrong. The trucks had turned back. Only the car, a Falcon, had showed up.

The driver of the Falcon informed the guerrilla leaders that the Austral airliner had been hijacked and was waiting on the tarmac at the Trelew airport.

They had to move quickly.

Ten of the inmates packed into the Falcon and took off for the airport.

Nobody left at the prison gate knew what to do now. There was no alternate plan.

Then, somebody had an idea: call for taxis.

Incredibly, three taxis showed up at the gate. Nineteen prisoners packed into the three cars.

Then Salvador made it twenty, by jumping on the back bumper of the last taxi.

He didn't have much to hold on to, and he knew that he wouldn't make it all the way from Rawson to the Trelew airport. At least, not at the speed they were going. But he was desperate and not thinking clearly.

He slapped his hands on the roof of the car to let them know he was there and the driver slowed down, but the other two taxis were already pulling away and Salvador could hear the prisoners inside yelling at the driver to go faster.

When the driver felt a gun pressed to the side of his head, he finally applied the gas and the car jolted forward. Salvador was able to hold on for only a couple of kilometres before he lost his grip. He was thrown onto the gravel and tumbled into the ditch. The taxi didn't even slow down.

He tried to stand, but his legs were cut and bruised. He could feel the gravel embedded in his skin from his kneecaps to his forehead.

A car pulled to the side of the road and stopped. A man got out of the car and rushed to support Salvador, then helped him to the car, gently laying him down on the back seat.

As soon as the man had pulled back on the road, Salvador slipped his bed-spring knife out from his boot and sat up in the seat.

The man looked in to the mirror, "Maybe you should lie down until I get you to the hospital in Trelew," he said. "You're pretty banged up. What the hell happened anyway?" He obviously had no idea that a mass prison escape was in progress.

"I crashed on my bicycle," Salvador lied. "I stashed it away before you showed up."

He looked ahead on the road and could see military trucks coming at them, rushing towards the prison. He lay back down and decided what he had to do to quickly fix the situation. He waited until the oncoming barrage of military vehicles had passed and then sat up.

"Something must be going on," the man observed. "That looked like the entire Argentine army."

"Maybe something at the prison," Salvador suggested, as he turned the bedspring in his hand. His adrenalin was working overtime, keeping him on an excited high and unaware of pain.

"Who knows what the military is doing these days," the man said looking at the rear view mirror. "I'm sure they're making somebody's life miserable."

"That's for sure," Salvador agreed.

"I'm going to get you to a doctor," the man said in a friendly tone. "You must be in a lot of pain. I'll come back later and pick up your bicycle."

"Don't worry about it," Salvador waved him off. "You've done enough already."

"My name is Eduardo," the driver said. "What's yours?"

"My name doesn't matter," Salvador said. He had no intention of getting personal with this guy. Their lives would only intersect for a brief moment. He swiftly slid the knife up from behind and then brought it up and around to the driver's throat. "Pull over," he ordered.

Eduardo did as he was told. When the car stopped, he turned his head as much as the sharp point would allow and said, "There's no need for this. I am trying to help you."

"You are helping me," Salvador replied. "I needed a car and everything else you have. And now I have it."

"Okay, then just take what you want and get the knife away from my throat. I have a ten-year-old daughter who has no mother."

Salvador couldn't resist another rush like the one he'd gotten from shooting the guard. He pushed the sharpened steel point as hard as he could and drove the bed frame leg completely into Eduardo's neck. The taxi driver's eyes bugged out as air and blood escaped from around the prison-made dagger.

"Now she has no father."

———

Esteban turned on the television and dropped heavily onto his couch when he finally got home. It had been the worst day of his life. First the escape, then Juan shot and killed, then pistol-whipping Salvador Juárez, then hiding in the electrical room for three hours, then the military arriving and taking control of the prison, then being held by the military and interrogated. In the end, he had had no food or water for sixteen hours. He was too exhausted to make anything to eat. He still had to tell his sister about Juan, and he had no idea if the escape was a success, or what had happened to Salvador Juárez.

The television news came on with a special report about the escape. The ten inmates who took the Falcon to the airport had got on the hijacked airliner and flown to Chile. Another nineteen inmates had arrived by taxi minutes after the plane took off and were stranded at the terminal. They took hostages and held a press conference before surrendering to the army. They had a judge verify their physical condition before they were taken back in custody and probably tortured. They also wanted their lawyers and reporters from the news media as witnesses.

The television showed a good view of all nineteen inmates standing shoulder to shoulder at the terminal. Esteban knew all of them. He liked all of them. He felt sorry for them.

He knew that Salvador Juárez was one of the thirty inmates missing from the prison, so he looked closely at them. Salvador was not one of the nineteen at the airport. Esteban was pretty sure that he hadn't killed Salvador and was also fairly confident that Salvador was not one of the ten who had made it to Chile.

Where had Salvador Juárez gone?

He was too exhausted to think about it. The news had gone on to an unrelated story of a taxi driver found murdered on the side of the road outside Rawson. *What is the country coming to?* Esteban turned off the television and went to bed. He would deal with it all tomorrow.

CHAPTER FOUR

August 23, 1972
San Carlos de Bariloche, Argentina

Salvador was driving his fifth stolen car, a white 1970 Fiat sedan, through a blinding snow storm along Nahuel Huapi Lake towards San Carlos de Bariloche when the news came on the radio. Bariloche was an Alpen-like ski resort town in the foothills of the Andes, close to the Chilean border, where more than a few Nazis had chosen to live out their lives quietly. Salvador figured they must have done their research and decided it was a good place to lay low for awhile. Now, with the icy wind blowing the needle-like snow horizontal and the inside of the car below freezing, he questioned the Nazi's choice.

But the news on the radio warmed his soul. The ten prisoners in the Falcon had taken off in the plane and made it safely to Chile. Negotiations were taking place with the governments of Chile and Argentina to have them returned. And, as it turned out, Salvador had been the only prisoner from the taxis to survive. All three taxis missed the plane by minutes. The nineteen escapees had taken hostages at the airport terminal and, after a lengthy press conference, had given themselves up to the government forces. They had been taken on a bus from the airport to a remote naval base, where yesterday, the radio reported they had all attempted to escape and were killed in a shootout. Salvador didn't believe there had been a shootout. He knew they had all been executed.

I am truly blessed. He laughed to himself. *I'm above everyone else.*

At that moment, Salvador had a vivid awareness of the man he was and would be. He would be a legend. An icon. He would even stand above Ché. He would be allusive and he would have money. Women would want him and no man would get in his way.

Suddenly he felt a sharp pain from the raw bruise on the right side of his head. He took the pill bottle from his jacket pocket and downed three more aspirins. The injury that the *yuga*, Esteban Lopez, had inflicted with the butt of his gun was beginning to get infected and in need of medical attention. It was a wound that would leave a scar. A wound Salvador would not easily forget.

PART TWO
SEVEN DAYS IN ARGENTINA

To convince oneself that one has a right to live decently takes time.
Evita Peron

CHAPTER ONE

December 16, 2001
Wet'suwet'en Nation
Northern British Columbia, Canada

Leonard Frank sat cross-legged in the tiny canvas-covered sweat lodge, elbow to elbow with seven others. He wore only jogging pants cut off at the knees, and in his hands he clutched a wad of fresh sage, which Old Man had given him for "protection." His solid, angular facial features were frozen expressionless. His wavy black hair was damp and finger-combed straight back, and shiny balls of sweat formed like beadwork across his brown chest. He appeared strong and wise.

But, on the inside, Leonard felt weak and ignorant. He was the only person in the close quarters that had not done a sweat before and the only one who had no experience in confronting and addressing the shadows slithering in the corridors of the soul. He had, however, entered with an open mind and good intentions, as instructed by Old Man and promised to Christine. He was already feeling his true self. Something that he had not felt since he was a boy.

Only his sister, Christine, knew him well enough to see below the surface. Leonard had made several good friends in thirty years of fire-fighting, but he bared his soul to nobody. Even his girlfriend was not a close friend. He only allowed others, including his girlfriend, to scratch the surface. It was convenient most people didn't care to dig too deeply into the psyche of others anyway. With fire fighters, it's all about the here and now, and with a girlfriend, it's all about what could be. He didn't know anything about what was going on inside them, and they didn't know what was going on inside him. Leonard was comfortable with that attitude. It was all those inside things that made life so complicated. Don't expose yours and I won't expose mine.

Several weeks earlier, Christine had taken part in a sweat lodge ceremony as research for a newspaper article. She'd got all hot and heavy on the ceremony and the wisdom of the medicine man. Christine recognized that Leonard would feel an affinity for Old Man because she knew Leonard missed the culture of his childhood and the "old ways," even if he never complained. Though he had been at odds with his younger sister for over forty years, he knew that nobody understood him better and nobody cared for him more. His sister, in her typical conniving ways, had arranged for Leonard to take her fishing, which he hated to do because she never actually fished as much as she talked, and then she showed up at his house with an ancient Cree medicine man, introduced him simply and aptly as Old Man and immediately left the two men alone, saying she had to meet somebody for a newspaper interview.

At first it was awkward, but Old Man had a deadpan sense of humour and a sharp wit that Leonard appreciated immediately. His ninety years had not taken as much away from him as it had given. He made Leonard think of his father and about what kind of elder he would have been if he had been able to grow old. Eventually, after they'd spent many *fishing* days together, Old Man learned the history of Leonard Frank and began talking about the need to heal the scars inside the soul. Leonard listened but was reluctant to admit there were any scars, there were only questions that needed to be answered, and possibly people who should be held accountable.

Old Man had grinned and replied that after thirty years, those questions and those people were the scars. Finally the Cree medicine man, using his wisdom and tact, had *converted* Leonard and prepared him to open himself for healing and take part in a sweat ceremony.

Old Man was on Leonard's right side, at the north point of the sweat lodge, singing a medicine song. He also sat cross-legged and also wore only shorts. His skin was pale, and it sagged from his bones. His wet grey hair hung from his skull like silver string down to his shoulders.

He was called Old Man because he was the oldest of his family line. Also, he was the wisest.

In addition to Leonard and Old Man, four women and two young men huddled inside the small canvas bubble, which, as Old Man had explained, represented the womb of Grandmother Earth. The men sat on one side and the women on the other. Leonard knew Bobby George, who held the ceremonial role of the doorkeeper, the person who allowed people through the canvas flap. He had hired the stocky young man on several forest fires. He was excellent a chainsaw operator and a leader among his peers.

Leonard didn't know the other young man, or any of the four women. Two of the women were young, probably in their twenties, and the other two were middle-aged. He had seen them all around town, but because he was a Carrier and not a member of the local First Nation, he wasn't part of the social network. He wasn't related to any of them, and he didn't live on the reserve. But he felt welcome here.

The most difficult part of the ceremony for Leonard was over. They had passed the pipe in a circle and, before each person smoked, they'd offered a prayer out loud for self, for others and for the release of pain and suffering. Each prayer ended with the phrase "...all my relations." It was a simple statement, as Old man had explained earlier, to be used when entering and leaving the sweat lodge and after your personal prayer to acknowledge connection to Grandmother Earth and to show honour for all living things.

The others mostly prayed for relatives who were on the Black Road of alcohol, or drugs.

Leonard's personal prayer was simple. He prayed for his sister Rosie.

It wasn't so bad saying the prayer out loud in front of others, and Leonard was actually feeling pretty good, as though he'd released some pressure. And he was surprised to find that he was feeling a strong spiritual energy flowing in the sweat lodge as well as the combined spiritual strength of all those present. It occurred to him that maybe all those monks he had seen on television chanting together might have the right idea. Before this moment, he had perceived each monk as lacking an individual personality, but now he understood that they were connecting themselves to gain strength and create spiritual energy.

Old Man continued to sing as he dipped a spruce bough into a galvanized pail of water and shook it over the red hot lava rocks. White steam exploded from the rocks like a shot of magic smoke uniting all the elements in life. Leonard pressed the fresh sage against his lips in search of cool air. Everything had meaning. Old Man had specially chosen and placed each rock in the depression at the centre. Four rocks were placed in the four directions and sprinkled with sage and sweet grass. Old Man's singing took on higher and louder notes as the air in the sweat lodge became wavy with the rising hot steam.

The searing heat expanded in Leonard's chest. Sweat rolled freely down his face and its salt burned his lips. He closed his eyes and felt lightness. He accepted the intense heat and drifted with Old Man's singing. The Cree words were not unlike his native tongue, the Carrier language, and he allowed his soul to ride with the sound waves and his body to flow with the heat waves. The energy current, strong and swift, quickly took him to another place, to the underworld of dreams.

He found himself standing on a dirt road, holding his little sister's hand. Behind them were the red brick buildings of the school, rising from the landscape like terracotta tombstones. A car was driving towards the horizon slowly. Their older sister, Rosie, was in the back seat and turned to look at them. She seemed sad, but she wasn't crying. Rosie never cried. She never had a reason to cry before the residential school.

She simply looked like a bug on a leaf, floating helplessly downstream.

The car seemed to take forever to drive away. It wasn't getting further down the road. It was just slowly disappearing in the wake of lifting brown dust.

Leonard felt helpless, as if he didn't exist.

He didn't want to exist.

He felt guilt freezing the blood in his veins.

He had let his sister be taken away. He had failed her.

Just before the car had completely disappeared in the rising cloud of dust, the driver turned. Leonard could see his silhouette.

It was the priest.

Leonard cried out, "No!"

His sudden outburst startled the others, stopped Old Man in mid-song and immediately brought Leonard back to the sweat lodge and the here and now. Old Man continued singing as the air cooled. Leonard relaxed, closed his eyes and concentrated on breathing.

When Old Man's medicine song came to an end, Bobby lifted the canvas flap for the fourth and final exit, and each person crawled out acknowledging "all my relations" while passing through the flap.

"All my relations," Leonard echoed as he crawled out through the flap last.

The morning sun was just peeking over the horizon, and the first light turned a layer of clouds red from the bottom up. The brightly painted reserve houses, with their active chimneys, looked like smoking flowers sprouting through the snow-covered yards. Two ravens, their feathers puffed out to insulate against the subzero air, squawked from the back of an abandoned pickup truck.

"That was great," Leonard said as he slipped into his parka. "We'll have to do it again sometime."

Old Man stood by the fire used to heat the rocks, his hands held out to the rising warmth, his eyes on the sunrise. Steam lifting from his wet silver hair gave the impression that he was present in the spirit world and the physical world at the same time. "Healing is like the river, Lenny. It's always moving and cleansing. Every once in awhile you have to jump right in, get wet and move along. Get clean."

"Hey, sorry about the sudden outburst in there. I kind of had a bad dream."

Old Man shrugged. "Happens all the time," he said. "And it scares the crap out of me every time."

The six other participants of the sweat giggled at the remark.

"Well, I have to get to work. I'm late already."

Old Man let out a soft chuckle and indicated the winter environment around them. "Yes, we wouldn't want any wildfires to get out of control today."

"Life is one wildfire after another," Leonard said with a grin.

"Seek and ye shall find," Old Man warned.

"Hey, I don't go looking for problems," Leonard protested. "Other people create problems. The government creates problems."

Old man held up a finger, "But you are the one that holds the problem."

"That's right," Leonard agreed. "And there lies my problem."

Old Man smiled and rubbed his hands together. "If you can hold it," he said, opening his hands with the palms down, "then you can let it go."

The six others all nodded, as if they had taken his advice and it had worked.

Leonard zipped up his parka and buried his hands deep into the warm pockets. "I wish it was that easy," he said.

Leonard had to drive home, take a shower, dress and drive to work. He would be late by a half hour at least. It didn't really matter, Old Man's sarcasm was not misplaced; there would be no wildfires today, in the middle of winter. And besides, it was the last day of work before Christmas holidays. Most civil servants in the small town wouldn't even show up for work, but Leonard didn't get a year-round career job with the Ministry of Forests by not showing up when he was being paid. Ever since he was eighteen years old and was chosen for a three-man Initial Attack crew, he showed up on time and ready. Five years later, he was chosen to be on the first specialty Initial Attack crew, which rappelled down ropes from helicopters into fires that burned in inaccessible locations. He was a good fire-fighter back then, and now, at forty-seven years old, he was probably the best Fire Behaviour Specialist in the province and a major innovator in fighting fire with fire.

The hot shower felt especially good after having done the sweat first thing in the morning. Leonard decided he would try to do the sweat regularly. Christine was right: although Leonard hated to admit it, he did feel better in many ways. Even with the strange excerpt from his past and those feelings of guilt and helplessness, he now felt more connected to himself and everything else, and light on his feet. *Maybe that's what healing is*, he thought. Leonard didn't like the word healing when it was applied to him. It made him sound weak and vulnerable, and Leonard Frank was anything but weak and vulnerable; more like strong and unaffected. But that was on the outside. On the inside, a demon always squirmed and twisted and gnawed at Leonard's subconscious. Occasionally it surfaced, with a nasty disposition, especially when Leonard was tired or frustrated. It was the thing that needed healing.

———

As soon as he stepped into the office, Leonard could tell something was up. His boss, Gord Hutchins, was leaning against the front counter, holding his coffee cup, just watching the door, as if waiting for Leonard.

"Hey, Boss. Sorry I'm late."

"I wasn't sure that you would even show up." Gord poured another cup of coffee, added two sugars and handed it to Leonard. "But I'm glad you did."

Leonard sipped the coffee as if he suspected it might be poisoned. "You looked like you were staring at the door, waiting for me to walk through it. That tells me you are going to pass off something to me that you don't want. Probably some kind of workload analysis bullshit report."

Gord laughed. "What're you talking about? You know I wouldn't pass off any bullshit to you. In fact, you could say I have kind of a Christmas present for you, in recognition of all your years of service."

"Okay, now I *know* you have some bullshit for me." Leonard put down his coffee and opened his arms. "Let me have it."

Gord sat down behind his desk and said one word. "Argentina."

Leonard thought for a second, and then shook his head. "What the hell does that mean? Is it code for something? Are you expecting a reply? How about … Bolivia?"

"I've got a paid trip for you to Argentina."

"What are you talking about? When? What for?"

"You remember that international development program? The exchange thing we had with Argentina? You applied for it."

"That was over a year ago. I didn't get in, probably because I don't speak a word of Spanish. I think Goodman got it. His Spanish is nearly fluent."

"Yeah, but he doesn't know shit about fire behaviour. Anyway, he's due to make his last trip to Buenos Aires, but his father died last night. He's on his way to Toronto now."

"So, reschedule the Argentina thing. Not a big deal. Why trade horses in midstream?"

"It's a federal program and required to be completed by the end of the year."

Leonard thought for a second. "The end of the year is less than two weeks away."

"Your plane leaves tonight."

"Well, that's not going to happen. You know I'm leaving tomorrow for Vancouver with Sonja."

Gord waved him off, "Yeah, yeah, I know, you're meeting her parents and it's going to be a joyful family gathering." Leonard was nodding along. "Well, you can still do that. You'll be back in Vancouver on Christmas morning."

"Oh, that will console Sonja," Leonard replied sarcastically. "You know she'll go ballistic if I don't do exactly what I'm supposed to do, starting the second I get off work this afternoon."

Gord shook his head. "Knowing you as I have for the last twenty-something years, I have to ask you, Lenny, do you really give a shit? I've seen you with better women and blow it for less than an opportunity to go to Argentina. You've only been with this lady for three months, you don't even live with her, and she already has her claws around your throat. She'll never last the next fire season. Cut your losses." The phone on his desk rang as if on cue. "That'll be headquarters, and they need an answer."

"Man, she'll be so pissed off."

The phone rang again. "It's summertime in Argentina. Think of beautiful Latinas in summer dresses. You can't beat a Latina ass."

"Home wrecker."

Gord snatched up the phone. "Fire Centre, Hutchins... Yes, he'll go...Okay...Okay...Okay, I'll tell him." He put the phone back in its place. "It's all set. Your ticket will be waiting for you at check in. Your contact in Argentina will meet you at the airport in Buenos Aires. A briefing package is being emailed to you as we speak. And I guess they are having some kind of economic crisis there right now, so they advise to bring U.S. cash and get receipts."

"Jesus, I can't believe how fast my life can change. Five minutes ago I was going to Vancouver with my girlfriend. Now, I'm going to Argentina and I don't have a girlfriend."

"You don't have to thank me, Lenny. The Lord works in mysterious ways."

"I wasn't planning on thanking you."

Gord laughed, "Oh, that will come later." He raised his coffee cup in a toast, "Give my best Christmas wishes to what's-her-name!"

"Sonja," Leonard replied. "Her name is Sonja."

"Well. Sonja," Gord held his cup higher, "*Feliz Navidad.*"

Leonard found himself clinking Gord's coffee cup and drinking to the toast. "I'll pass on your Christmas greeting," he said. "She'll be touched."

———

A few hours later, when Leonard was in his bedroom packing for the trip, the phone rang. In the split-second after he answered, he realized it was time to pass on the Christmas news.

Sonja seemed surprised when he answered. "Lenny? What are you doing home?" Her Slavic accent highlighted her suspicious tone. "I was just going to leave a message for you to remember to pick up Mother's present."

"Yeah, Honey, I was just going to call you. I've had a change in plans." Leonard tensed up for what he knew would come.

There was a quick knock on the front door and Christine stuck her head in. "Hey, Bro..." She saw he was on the phone and stopped at the doorway.

Sonja went right on the attack. "What the fuck are you talking about?" she spoke so loud that Leonard had to move the phone from his ear, and Christine could hear her from the other side of the room. "Change of fucking plans?"

"Yeah, Bob Goodman's father died yesterday. I have to go to Argentina as his replacement. But I'll be back Christmas day."

"Argentina!" Sonja was incredulous. "Listen to me, Sweetheart, I don't give a shit if Bob Goodman's entire family was fucking massacred by the Argentina fucking cartel. If you don't leave with me tomorrow, then Adios! And fuck you!"

"But there's nothing…" Leonard stopped his lame excuse as he realized he was talking to a dial tone and dropped the phone next to his suitcase on the bed.

Christine strode into the bedroom as if it was hers. "She's a total bitch anyway. Good riddance." She flopped down on Leonard's bed. For a woman in her mid-forties, Christine carried herself as if she had got stuck at around twenty. And physically she looked more twenty than forty. Her small body in tight jeans and sweatshirt, her big black hair on the edge of being committed to dreadlocks and her don't-give-a-shit attitude all pointed to college student. It got her more than a few nights of pleasure with men half her age. She tapped Leonard's suitcase. "So, you're going to Argentina now?"

"Yeah, is that a problem?" Leonard straightened the suitcase and continued to pack. "Can you still watch the place?"

"Vancouver, Argentina, makes no difference to me." Christine sounded nonchalant. "This place is Party Central for the next week, regardless of where you are. But, what's-her-name didn't seem like she was onside."

"Sonja. Her name was Sonja." Leonard noticed he was already speaking of her in the past tense.

Christine sat up on the bed. "What's with Argentina, anyway? Didn't you get turned down last year for that?"

"Well, things change. A time-locked budget here, a death there and the next thing I know, I'm on my way to South America." Leonard closed the suitcase and zipped it up. There was a blue file on the bed, and he picked it up. "Do you know what this is?"

Christine didn't look at the file; she got up from the bed, went to the dresser and picked up a framed photograph. It was a black-and-white of Leonard, Christine and Rosie when they had first arrived at the residential school with their school clothes and bowl-shape haircuts. Behind them stood a tall, dark priest. His eyes looked hard and mean. The girls were separated from the boys after the picture was taken, and it was the last time Christine was near Leonard until he snuck into the girl's dormitory and they ran away. It was three nights after Leonard saw Rosie in the back of a car being driven away.

"Why do you keep this picture?" she asked him.

Leonard took it from her and put it back on the dresser. "It's the only picture I have of her, and it's the last time we were all together."

"Well, you could at least crop out the asshole priest."

"It helps me to remember him also."

"That's what that blue file is, isn't it? It's the file on Father Ricardo."

"That investigator I hired, the one you slept with, tracked Ricardo to Buenos Aires. Then I ran out of money."

"And then my attention span with him ran out. He was kind of geeky for a private investigator. I was hoping the next one you hired would be a little more, ah … manly."

"I'll try my best. Anyway, I'm taking the file with me. Maybe I'll have time to do a little investigating on my own."

"Jesus, Leonard, it's been like more than thirty years! All we know is that back then Ricardo took a flight from Santiago to Buenos Aires. He could have got on another connecting flight fifteen minutes later to anywhere in the world. And isn't Buenos Aires a city of more than ten million people? And don't they all speak a language you don't speak?"

"Okay, okay." Leonard tossed the file back on the bed and sat down. "It's a shot in the dark, but at least it's doing something. It seems like I haven't done anything for so long now. I don't want to give up. Maybe I could hire an investigator there."

Christine put her fingers in his hair and scratched his scalp, something she had done since they were kids. "You've done everything you could, Leonard. Enjoy your few days there. Find a cute South American salsa dancing whore and have a good time. Forget that bitch Sonja. Did I tell you I had a feeling about her? And, forget Father-fucking-Ricardo, I'm sure somebody has killed him by now. At least I hope so."

"If I give up with Ricardo, I'm giving up on Rosie."

"I know what you mean." Christine bit her lip. "You can't do that." Then she smiled like the troublemaker she was. "But, what do you think about the salsa dancing whore?"

Leonard grinned. "I won't rule it out."

CHAPTER TWO

Day One
December 18, 2001
Buenos Aires, Argentina

Marcela Cruz lay sprawled on her back across her bed. Only a light sheet covered her body, creating a topographic map of her lissom peaks and valleys. At thirty-six years of age and after giving birth, she still had the body of a lean fourteen-year-old boy. Her first thought as she opened her eyes was *I need to get my hair cut short*. The heat and humidity of Buenos Aires around Christmas was always suffocating, even in the morning. Her hair fell only just to her shoulders. It was not nearly as long as Olivia's, but it was thick and black, and soaked up heat. Or perhaps she just wanted to get it cut for a change. Maybe she would get it cut real short. Her hands moved involuntarily to cover her nipples. No, if she cut it short she would definitely look like a fourteen-year-old boy.

She turned and looked at the CD player's digital clock on the bedside table. 6:59. She stared at the clock for a few more seconds, until it turned to 7:00, and the CD player automatically clicked on with Gloria Estefan's "Mi Tierra" at high volume.

"Good morning, daughter," Marcela spoke out loudly over the music. "Did you sleep well?" There was no reply from the bedroom across the hallway. She forced herself up to a sitting position, wiped the sleep from her eyes and took a couple of breaths. As her brain awakened, the realities of the world outside crept into her consciousness. She quickly shook off those thoughts and got out of bed, walked naked across the hallway and stuck her head in her seventeen-year-old daughter's room. Olivia, face down in her bed, held a pillow over her head to block out the loud and lively salsa.

"Good morning, *hija*." Marcela attempted to sound enthusiastic. "It's time for another beautiful day."

Olivia gripped the pillow tighter to her ears.

Marcela shuffled her way to the bathroom, her narrow hips just catching a bit of Gloria's beat. By the time she had showered, her hips had woken up and she danced out of the bathroom Carmen Miranda-style, in bra and panties and a towel on her head. She shook and danced her way out of the bathroom, past the kitchen, where Olivia, already dressed in her school uniform, was putting a kettle on the stove, and danced on down the hallway, stopping for a quick shake to the congas. Back in her bedroom, she turned down the music and slipped into a conservative blue skirt and a white silk blouse. As she looked in the mirror brushing out the tangles in her hair, she decided she would definitely get her hair cut.

"Do you think I should get my hair cut?" she asked Olivia as she sat at the kitchen table for their morning ritual of sharing *maté,* the strong Argentine tea, and toast.

Olivia appeared thoughtful and fingered her own hair which, along with her body, was much longer and a lighter shade than her mother's. "Well, if it's between a hair cut and getting a boob job, I'd do the boob job."

"Thanks. That's exactly what I was wondering."

"I was joking. I like your hair the way it is. Maybe get a trim."

"Did the demonstrators keep you up all night with all the pots and pans banging?" she asked.

Olivia sipped the *maté* through the *bombilla*, a stainless steel straw, until she had achieved a sucking air sound, then poured in more hot water and handed it to her mother. "No," she said, "I'm getting used to it now. It's been a few nights almost non-stop, and I have earplugs if it really bothers me."

Marcela sucked on the *bombilla* and passed it back. "Well," she said firmly, "I don't like the way things are going. The banks are freezing all the accounts and closing their doors. People aren't going to like that. Things are going to get violent. I want you to stay away from any demonstrations."

Olivia shrugged and buttered a slice of toast, like the disinterested seventeen-year-old she was. "This isn't 1977, Mother, and we don't have a military government. There are always demonstrations." She gave the buttered toast to Marcela. "Don't worry."

Marcela looked hard at Olivia, directly into her eyes, making sure her daughter understood that this was serious. "It's my destiny to worry, *hija*, and I have good reasons to worry now. These are not your usual demonstrations. It's not just the professional picketers out there, it's everybody. The government can't survive this."

Olivia shrugged and sipped *maté*. "Well, I'll be careful. I have no desire to get involved."

"We are all involved, whether you desire it or not." Marcela stood up from the table and picked up her handbag. "I'll see you here when I get back from work. You still have one last test to study for."

Olivia let out an exaggerated sigh. "Mother," she pleaded, "it's the English test. I don't need to study."

"That sounds way too confident, which means that you'd better study for sure."

"Pedro asked me to go with him on his deliveries after school."

"Tell him some other time. I'll see you here when I get back from work." Marcela's voice was firm, leaving no room for debate. "Now, let's go, before the demonstrations shut down everything."

Out on the street it was an entirely different environment from the private sanctuary of their little apartment. Large crowds of demonstrators had already assembled. *Maybe they have been assembled all night,* Marcela thought. They were shoulder to shoulder and moved from all directions towards the Avenida de Mayo. They banged pans together and chanted slogans. Marcela took Olivia's hand and made her way through the crowds down to the underground station.

When they arrived at the third stop, where Olivia got off for her school, they kissed, and Marcela recounted her after-school instructions. Olivia replied with a flippant wave of her hand and left the subway car just before the doors slid shut.

Marcela went two more stops to reach the Ministry of Environment building. The demonstrations were far from this area of the city, and coming out of the underground here was like stepping into another country. Flowers were blooming, birds were singing and people carried on with life. On the surface, at least, life seemed normal.

She wasn't surprised. *What else can you do?*

The vibrant blond receptionist greeted Marcela as soon as she entered the building. "Guess what happened last night?" she said, bubbling with excitement and pulling at Marcela's arm.

"Let's see, Mariana. Ricky Martin stopped by your apartment and had some kind of bizarre sex with you."

Mariana's soft, puffy face froze, and she put her hand to her mouth. "That's scary," she whispered. "Only it wasn't Ricky Martin, it was that accountant I was telling you about."

"That's probably already more than I want to know about your date last night."

"I'll tell you the juicy parts later. Right now, Diego wants to see you and he has that hot chauffer, Ernesto, with him."

"What's going on?"

Mariana shook her head. "I have no idea. The boss has been locked in his office and on the phone since the country went bankrupt."

Marcela took a breath, "Well, hopefully I still have a job."

As soon as she stepped into his office, Marcela could see that Diego was not at his usual level of self-confidence and personal grooming. Normally his well-cut grey hair, silver-framed glasses and flawless brown skin gave him that executive better-than-you appearance. But now his hair was messed, and his eyes were tired, and he had that workingman's don't-fuck-with-me appearance. The chauffeur sat quietly to his side. A handsome man in his early twenties, the chauffeur had his black hair slicked back. He wore black pants and a white shirt with a black tie.

Diego got right to the point. "I have a job for you for the next week. I was just giving instructions to Ernesto, your driver."

Marcela glanced at the chauffeur, who sat up a little straighter. "I already have enough work to fill the next ten weeks," she said. "And none of it requires a driver."

"Yes," Diego sighed, "I know, but this is more immediate and I'm busy trying to keep our jobs alive. I want you to take over and complete the Canada project. I've already done all the leg work with Bob Goodman. You remember Bob?"

Marcela nodded, "Yes, you guys were really getting some serious work done." Her sarcasm was not disguised.

Diego ignored her tone. "Bob's father has died and he's off the project. Another guy is coming now, a Frank Leonard - or Leonard Frank, I'm not sure which. The final report should only take you and him a day to finish up."

Marcela shrugged. "I guess I can spare a day at some point."

Diego took off his glasses. "The problem is that he will be here a week. I need you to keep him occupied."

Marcela was already shaking her head. "A week! No way!"

Diego sat back in his leather chair. "Show him around the city, introduce him to some of our people, and organize a dinner, that kind of thing. Just keep him away from the demonstrations and out of trouble."

Marcela continued to shake her head. "I don't do that liaison shit. I do fire science. I'm not good at public relations or entertaining or making small talk. You know that. If he's left with me, Canada will probably break off diplomatic ties with Argentina. And besides, this is not a good time for me. I have family responsibilities. "

Diego was tapping his fingers on his desk. Finally he said, "I get the impression that you have the impression that I am asking you to do this."

"When does this Mr. Leonard, or Mr. Frank, or whatever his name is, arrive?"

"Today. Right now. Ernesto here will drive you to the airport to meet him."

"No, no, no!" Marcela was adamant now, and her raised hands expressed that along with the firm tone of her voice. "Absolutely not! I have my daughter to take care of, and I have to try to deal with this banking mess and see if I can get my money from the frozen accounts. I have no time to lead around a gringo bureaucrat. No sir, I am sorry, truly, but you'll have to get somebody else." Marcela's brown eyes suddenly lit up. "Have Mariana do it! It will be like a date for her. She would probably even sleep with him."

Diego was still tapping. "Mariana doesn't speak English. Besides she is too stupid to do this."

"Well, I'm *not* stupid enough to do it."

Diego looked at his watch. "You have about forty-five minutes to be at the arrival gate at Ezeiza airport." He turned to the driver. "Ernesto, how long does it take to drive to Ezeiza airport?"

The young man shrugged, "About forty minutes, sir."

"Then you two had better get going. Bring him here directly from the airport."

Marcela's face tensed with anger. "You can be sure that I will bring him directly here, to you."

——

Marcela made a quick sign with a felt pen and cardboard, *FRANK LEONARD*. She held it at chest level towards the stream of travelers flowing through the Customs turnstile. She had an image in her head of the type of person she was looking for: a white man, approximately fifty years old, well-trimmed grey hair, probably a Hawaiian shirt. A gringo Diego.

Suddenly she noticed a man standing in front of her, smiling. Of medium height, he was solidly built, and had dark skin and wavy black hair combed straight back. His face displayed solid, angular features and his eyes were almond-shaped. His age could have been thirty-five, or fifty. He had the look and the aura of a Sherpa from Nepal.

"*Hola*," he said, maintaining his smile and offering his hand to shake, "*Yo soy* Leonard Frank. And that's about all the Spanish I know."

"Oh!" Marcela dropped her sign and shook his hand. "I was expecting somebody more—"

"White?" he offered.

"Well, yes." she admitted. "More Anglo-looking, anyway."

He picked up the sign and pointed to the name. "It's Leonard Frank."

Marcela suddenly felt embarrassed. "Sorry," she apologized. "My boss wasn't sure, so I guessed."

"It's the kind of name a Native gets when white men couldn't pronounce our real names. They registered our ancestors with names they could pronounce, so now we have Jim Bob, Jackie Johnnie and Leonard Frank. Not very imaginative."

"No, but I suppose it could have been worse," Marcela said. "You could have been Bob Shithead." She smiled, "I'm Marcela Cruz, from the Ministry of Environment."

Leonard smiled back. *"Mucho gusto,* Marcela Cruz."

Realizing that perhaps they had been holding the handshake a bit too long, they broke grip at the same time. "Our driver is waiting outside," Marcela said quickly. "We'll go to the office and get you situated. You must be hungry and tired."

"No," Leonard said. "I'm fine."

Marcela made her way through the airport, with Leonard right behind her, much faster than she had to go. She found that she felt nervous and a little, well yes, stupid. Once they were out of the coolness of the terminal and into the startling heat and humidity, she heard Leonard gasp. She stopped and asked, "Are you okay?"

Leonard waved her off. "Yes, fine, thanks. Just had to catch my breath. Yesterday I was driving in a snowstorm in sub-zero temperatures. This heat is kind of a shock."

Ernesto was waiting with the car near the line of taxis. He was leaning casually on the car, talking to a couple of pretty teenage girls, laughing and impressing them. When he saw Marcela approaching, he quickly gave the girls his business card and excused himself. The girls continued down the sidewalk, giggling and looking at the card as if it were a celebrity's autograph. Walking to the rear of the car, Ernesto opened the trunk and then the back door. Putting on a huge smile, he stood at attention.

Leonard didn't wait for an introduction. *"Hola, yo soy* Leonard Frank." He offered his hand to shake.

Ernesto ignored the handshake and gave Leonard the customary Argentine greeting, a hug and a kiss on the cheek, instantly making Leonard visibly uncomfortable. Marcela rolled her eyes. Ernesto should have known that North Americans didn't do the kiss-on-the-cheek thing.

"I'm Ernesto de Salvo, government chauffeur extraordinaire," he said, surprising Marcela by speaking perfect English. "And I'm definitely not gay. That's the traditional Argentine greeting. I was also chauffeur for Bob Goodman. He depended on me for cultural info and insisted we be casual with each other." He took Leonard's suitcase and put it in the trunk.

"Well, I plan to follow in his footsteps," Leonard said. "Let's not change a thing."

As Ernesto manoeuvred the car into the traffic leaving the airport, he had the radio turned a bit too loud and drove just a bit too fast for Marcela to be comfortable. "I thought all Canadians were Anglo, or maybe French types," he said looking into the mirror.

"Well, I'm a First Nations Canadian - aboriginal, native, Indian, however you want to say it." Leonard had to speak loudly to be heard above the music.

"Cool! Like a Mohawk, or an Apache?"

"Something like that. Carrier actually."

"I'm part native myself," Ernesto said proudly to the rear-view mirror. "My grandmother was Mapuche."

Marcela had enough. "Turn that radio off!" she ordered in Spanish. "Jesus, how can you listen to this shit."

Ernesto turned the volume down. "It's Argentine rap. Pretty cool, eh, Mr. Frank? Experiencing the local culture. Hey, Chief, are you married, or have a serious girlfriend?"

Leonard was looking out the window at a couple of young Latina women in summer dresses walking arm in arm down the street. "No," he said, "I never married."

"Then you should be able to appreciate Buenos Aires." Ernesto grinned at the rear-view mirror. "But then, Bob Goodman told me that in Vancouver you could not have your eyes open and not have a beautiful woman in sight."

Leonard grinned back to the mirror. "That's probably true."

"I didn't know you spoke English," Marcela said to Ernesto suddenly in Spanish.

"There's a lot that you don't know about me," Ernesto replied in English with a wink to the mirror for Leonard.

"Well, speak less of it and be less casual. I expect you to be professional," Marcela said quickly in Spanish. She turned to Leonard and asked in English, "Are you aware of what's going on in Argentina right now, Mr. Frank?"

"Please call me Leonard, or Lenny. No, not really. I heard about some economic problems."

"Basically, the country just declared bankruptcy. Our banks have shut their doors and frozen our accounts. International banks, like Canadian banks, are taking their money and running, and our government is falling."

Leonard was quiet for a moment. Then he said, "That must be bad for you personally. I'm sorry. This is probably not the most convenient time for you to have to deal with me." He spoke in the same tone that he used with people who had just lost their home to a forest fire.

"Oh no," Marcela waved him off, ignoring Ernesto's raised eyebrow in the mirror. "I'm happy to do this."

"Well, don't feel you have to do too much. I can get around all right if you point me in the right direction."

Marcela was feeling confused and didn't know how to reply. An hour ago, she had been adamant about not entertaining the Canadian bureaucrat. Now she wasn't so sure. She had only known Leonard for twenty minutes, but she felt like she would like to get to know him more. He had a relaxed way about him and seemed easy to be around. And although she didn't want to admit it to herself, she was attracted to him in some way that she couldn't define. "Let's see what the boss has to say," she finally replied.

━━

Leonard wasn't sure if Diego was rising from his desk to greet him with a handshake or the Argentine hug and kiss, so he was ready for either. He relaxed when it turned out to be the handshake. After Marcela introduced them, they sat down and Diego got down to business. "I understand that you got this thing dropped on you just before Christmas holidays, Leonard. The death of Bob's father was very unfortunate."

Leonard shook off the sympathy, "It isn't a problem, Diego. I've looked at the file and it seems most of the work is done. And this is a great opportunity for me to see Buenos Aires."

"Unfortunately, you are seeing our country in a dark moment. Our economy is collapsing and taking the government with it. Or maybe it's the other way around. I'm sure you understand that since our department is funded by the government, I have some matters to attend to. Marcela has graciously volunteered to step in and assist you. She is a fire science expert. She will help with the report and get you set up with a motel and meals. I have assigned our car and driver to provide transportation."

"That's very generous, Mr. Gonzales."

Diego stood up, indicating the meeting was over, so Leonard and Marcela also stood. "I wish I could do more, Leonard." They shook hands again. "Don't let the unrest prevent you from seeing the beauty of our city. You have just caught us at a bad time."

When they were back at the car, Marcela insisted that Leonard sit in front with Ernesto to get a good view. They pulled out into the busy traffic with the rap music still too loud and Ernesto still driving too fast. "Ernesto, turn that shit off and slow down!" she commanded in Spanish.

Leonard was snapping pictures of the large gatherings of rowdy demonstrators, men and women, children and elders, banging pots and pans in the streets, many with bandanas covering their faces, some waving big sticks high above their heads. "These demonstrations are pretty large," he said with a hint of concern. "Any chance of violence?"

Marcela nodded. "You get this many people angry, and a bunch of young macho police with batons, guns and rubber bullets, and the potential for violence is definitely there. You'll have to be careful to avoid the large gatherings."

Police dressed in black, wearing bullet-proof vests and armed with batons and guns, formed lines in front of banks and government buildings. The scene reminded Leonard of a news broadcast he had seen as a teenager that left him completely frightened. "I remember watching television when Canada's prime minister proclaimed the War Measures Act in Canada in 1970 because the FLQ had kidnapped Quebec's

Minister of Labour and eventually killed him. The soldiers were everywhere. Why isn't the army involved here? I only see police."

"Leaders from the military government of the late seventies are still being prosecuted for their abuse of power back then, so I'm sure the military hierarchy today wants to distance itself from this situation. And the politicians know they can hide behind the actions of the police, even though the orders for the police come from the politicians. It would be difficult for the politicians to hide behind the military."

"Where are we going now?"

"I'll get you set up in a hotel not far from my apartment," Marcela said, "and you can get some rest. Tomorrow morning we'll pick you up and make a plan from there. It's too bad this wasn't better organized and at a better time. I have things to do tomorrow, so I won't be available for most of the day, and it's Ernesto's day off, but I will be able to set you up in the morning with things to do on a Sunday in Buenos Aires. You could do some local sightseeing."

Leonard stopped taking pictures and put his camera back in its case. "Don't worry about keeping me entertained, Marcela. I've done some travelling, I have my *Lonely Planet* Latin American Spanish book, and I can get around. And I have something I want to investigate a bit, probably at the Canadian embassy or maybe at a library."

Marcela quickly gave Ernesto some directions in Spanish, and then turned to Leonard. "You can tell me more about that in the morning. The embassy and the library will be closed tomorrow because it's Sunday, but we can talk and perhaps I will be able to help."

Leonard waved her off. "Hey, Marcela, I know it's a bad time for you right now. I can see that you got this dropped on you like I got it dropped on me, so don't feel you have to be my guide. We can do the report in one day. I've seen the notes. The rest of the time we can keep in touch and you can go about your business."

Marcela shifted uncomfortably in her seat. "You're right," she said. "This is not a good time and I did get this dropped on me out of nowhere this morning."

Ernesto had turned down a narrow city street and then pulled over to the curb in front of a small hotel. They all got out of the car, and while Marcela went to the front desk, Ernesto retrieved Leonard's suitcase from the back of the car.

"Hey, Chief," Ernesto said in a lowered voice as he handed the suitcase over. "I can set you up with pretty well anything that you desire. Don't hesitate to ask." He slipped a business card from his shirt pocket and gave it to Leonard. "Anything," he repeated, making sure that the word was understood.

Marcela finished securing a room and presented Leonard with the key. "It's 313 on the third floor. They have a bit of a breakfast down in the lobby in the morning."

"*Gracias*, Marcela."

"We'll come see you in the morning. Right now you should get some rest. You probably have jet lag. If you want to eat later, there are several kinds of places within a block or two."

After Marcela and Ernesto had driven away, Leonard went to his room. But not directly - he first had to learn that what the Argentines refer to as the third floor is what North Americans consider the fourth floor. A very kind and patient cleaning lady explained it several times before the point finally broke through the jet-lag. Eventually he found the room and wiggled the key in the lock to open the door. As soon as he entered, he dropped his suitcase and fell on the bed. There was a remote for the television attached to the headboard, so he pressed the red power button. A soccer game came alive on the small television attached high on the wall across from the bed. He kicked off his shoes and laid on his back, adjusted the pillow under his head and stared at the soccer game, listening to the passionate commentators and not understanding a word.

His thoughts turned quickly to his Argentine colleague. It surprised him that he had felt comfortable around Marcela immediately. Usually he went into a game-playing mode when he was communicating with a woman he was attracted to, but in a strange way it was as if they knew each other well. There had been no nervousness, no stupid fumbling conversation, no awkward dancing around each other with words.

He gave his head a shake. *What am I thinking? She is my colleague, not somebody I met at one of Christine's parties, and I'm only here for a few days. I have to concentrate on trying to find out something about Father Ricardo and getting this report finished. And besides, I am a forty-seven-year-old bachelor who can't maintain a relationship, and she's a thirty-something, smart and beautiful Latina, who could have any man she wanted. Let's get real.*

Finally, the twenty-eight gruelling hours of travelling, the five-hour time difference and the complete weather change caught up with him, and his consciousness drifted away in a single wave of weightlessness and sleep.

CHAPTER THREE

Day Two
December 19, 2001
Buenos Aires, Argentina

Leonard jumped to his feet and found himself opening the door before he was actually awake or sure that somebody really had knocked on the door. He was greeted by Ernesto, Marcela and a very pretty teenage girl. They all looked so fresh and awake that he suddenly felt very self-conscious about his sloppy, slept-in appearance and his sleepy eyes.

Marcela put her hand to her mouth. "Oh God, I forgot about the time change. We're too early."

Leonard waved her off. "No, not at all, come in. I didn't want to sleep all day." Leonard moved aside, and the three others crowed into the small room. "Make yourselves comfortable. I'll take a quick shower and change."

Ernesto looked down at the bed. "Well, at least you got your shoes off, Chief, even if you didn't get between the sheets."

Marcela indicated Olivia to Leonard. "Mister Frank, I would like to introduce to you my daughter Olivia."

Olivia, without a pause, gave Leonard a hug and a kiss on the cheek. "I am very happy to meet you, Mister Frank." She spoke English as if she were reading it from a textbook.

Leonard, a little embarrassed by his fumbling on the hug and kiss greeting, made a little bow. "*Mucho gusto*, Olivia, and please call me

Leonard." He was a bit stunned that Olivia was Marcela's daughter. He had never stopped to think that Marcela would have a husband and children. He pointed to the television that had been on all night, and was showing yet another soccer game. "There's a good soccer game on," he said. "I'll just be ten minutes."

"We call it football here," Ernesto said, "and this is a game we don't care about. Do you mind if I change the channel?"

"Ernesto," Marcela sighed, "just sit down and don't touch anything,"

When Leonard emerged from the bathroom fifteen minutes later, clean and refreshed, the television was showing a rock video. A screaming androgynous she-male, banging a loud triangular guitar, was surrounded by dancing, near-naked Latinas. Ernesto and Olivia were hypnotized by the repetitious beat and shaking asses, but Marcela was obviously irritated with it. Leonard went to his suitcase and took out a T-shirt featuring the logo of the Toronto Maple Leafs hockey team, a blue maple leaf. "Is the game over?"

"Yes," Ernesto replied, "and your team lost. Hey, nice shirt."

"It's a hockey team." Leonard didn't add that it was what his mother was wearing the last time he saw her.

"Oh right, Canadian, hockey. It makes sense."

"Can we go now?" Marcela asked.

"Okay," Leonard said, "I'm ready. What's on the agenda? We do a little breakfast thing, you point me in a direction and then you do your thing and I play *turista*?"

Marcela went to the remote and turned the loud television off. "That's pretty close, but first we have to take Olivia to choir practice. We'll go get a coffee while she is practising. I have a map of the city, and we can discuss and circle places that you might be interested in seeing. After we pick up Olivia, we will drop you off at a good place to access where you want to go, and then we'll come back and pick you up for supper."

"Oh no." Leonard held up his hands. "I'll be way lost by suppertime. You should have supper with your family. If you want to pick me up sometime tomorrow in the midmorning, we can reconnect then."

They dropped off Olivia in front of a very old stone church, and Marcela directed Ernesto to a cafe where they could sit at a table on the sidewalk and get coffee and pastries. It was a beautiful morning in Buenos Aires, not as humid as the day before, and Leonard was happy to sit outside and get some air.

Marcela spread a map on the table in the sunlight and smoothed it out. "So, what kind of places would you be interested in seeing, Mr. Frank?"

"Please, it's Leonard. Anybody who calls me Mr. Frank is somebody I have to be careful of, and I'm sure that you're not a threat, Miss—"

"It's Marcela, and no, I am definitely not a threat." She said it with a smile and tone that kept it light.

"Well, Marcela, I really don't know anything about Buenos Aires. It looks like a beautiful city."

"I can circle some nightspots," Ernesto blurted out.

"Yes," Marcela answered, "and then he'll know the places to avoid."

"I do have some things to look into while I'm here," Leonard said, "but it is Sunday and the Canadian embassy is probably closed too. I'll just wander around a bit, take some pictures and have a relaxing day."

"Well," Marcela offered, "Buenos Aires is known for its architecture, food and, of course, the tango." Marcela said.

"And its women," Ernesto added.

"I'll circle some places of interest, like La Boca, where the tango was born, San Telmo, another great tango area, and La Recoleta, where Evita Perón rests."

"Sounds great, circle them all."

A group of young ladies who sipped cold drinks a few tables down the sidewalk had caught Ernesto's attention and he excused himself. "Pardon me for a moment. I should say hello to my cousin."

"Cousin, my ass," Marcela scoffed. "Just don't wander out of sight."

As Ernesto left the table, Marcela caught Leonard smiling at her. "What?" she laughed. "Did I say something?"

"No, no, it's nothing." Leonard said, waving her off. "I was just amazed at how well you speak English."

"I watch a lot of television," she laughed. "Actually, I took it all through school and went to an English academy after school."

"Is that where you met Olivia's father?" Leonard immediately regretted what he said. It had nothing to do with what they were talking about.

Marcela looked slightly taken by the question. "No," she said.

Leonard was embarrassed. "I'm sorry, Marcela. That wasn't a proper question."

"No," she waved him off, "it's okay. Olivia's father was Argentine. He was killed in the Malvinas war the year she was born."

"Malvinas?" Leonard had never heard of Malvinas.

"The Falkland Islands War," she translated.

—

June 11, 1982
Plata Sector
Islas Malvinas, Argentina

Carlos Ortiz sat on the rocky edge of his foxhole, smoking a cigarette and gazing out at the rising moon. He was feeling lonely, cold and a bit frightened. He had been positioned, with a FAL rifle, on the western edge of what the islanders called Mount Longdon, in a hole blasted out of rock. Depression and cynicism had completely taken over, and he didn't care about Las Malvinas anymore. They could call it fucking Kelperland for all he cared. It didn't matter now. Most of the 1,800 resident islanders wanted the 20,000-plus British and the Argentines to fuck off anyway.

He had been on the island for nearly two months, the worst two months of his life. His regiment had been deployed from La Plata when the Argentine command realized that the British weren't going to take the recovery of Islas Malvinas sitting down. England had sent battleships loaded for war, aircraft carriers packed with Sea Harriers and an ocean liner full of elite commandos and parachute units. It didn't look like political negotiation was going to move along – NATO had passed a resolution calling for Argentina's complete withdrawal from the island and, since it had taken 150 years to recover the islands, Carlos knew that the Argentine command would not give it up easily.

For six weeks, they dug into the hills and rocky ridges west of Puerto Argentina and waited. They were allowed to walk into town once a week for a makeshift shower, but Carlos and many others were too weak and hungry to make the long walk more than twice in six weeks. He wore all the clothes he had and still he was freezing. His regiment arrived with the clothes they had been issued in La Plata for a Buenos Aires type of climate, and the only extra item they were issued for the frigid Malvinas winter was an Israeli-made anorak. Carlos was wet, cold and hungry every second of every day. There was virtually no food, only one small plastic tray per person per week, usually completely devoured on the first day. The winter weather was unrelenting, with horizontal rain and freezing wind. And the terrain was an inhabitable soggy, peaty, rocky hell.

Carlos knew that an overwhelming attack by professional British commandos was imminent; he just hoped that they didn't bring the fucking Gurkhas. One of the reservists had told him that the Gurkhas were the worst soldiers to go up against - they used scare tactics that left experienced warriors demoralized. It was said that they would sneak into enemy tents at night and slit every other person's throat. What chance would he have, with just over a year in the army as a conscript, against a full-time, professional fucking Gurkha? No chance! Maybe he would try to surrender before they could kill him. He had something to live for, something that was much more important than the recovery of Malvinas. Only a week before he was sent to war, his seventeen-year-old girlfriend had informed him that she was pregnant.

He had promised her that he would come back for her.

He tossed his cigarette butt into the water that had built up in the bottom of his foxhole and looked at his watch. It was almost 9:30. This was going to be a long night. Hunger knotted his stomach and he couldn't stop shaking from the cold. He doubted that they would see action, but he had to stay awake and keep his eyes open, because one of the officers had ordered the Rasit radar on the hill to be turned off so that the enemy wouldn't detect its emissions and take it out. Carlos thought that was stupid - the radar had saved their ass on previous nights. At least the forward observation artillery officer, Lieutenant Ramos, was out there to warn of any movement before it got to Carlos, and unlike Carlos he was a good soldier.

A quick little glint of moonlight reflection, nearly a kilometre in the distance, caught Carlos's eye. His vantage point was perched on the steep western slope, almost seventy metres above the wide-open lowland expanse, looking to the northwest. The lowland had hundreds of land mines planted into the grassy hummocks, but Carlos figured that it had been so wet and cold, that they would be frozen and thus inoperable. And, it was unlikely that the British would approach from this direction anyway; the terrain was both very difficult and very exposed. Even in the dim moonlight, Carlos could see the mountain eight kilometres away. If they did stage an attack from this direction, most likely it would be just before dawn, or in the daylight.

He strained his eyes in a squint, but he could see nothing more.

Suddenly, a burst of bright light and white smoke, half a kilometre in the distance, followed by a small explosion, lit up the sky and broke the night silence.

A mine. Somebody had tripped a land mine!

Carlos dropped down into his foxhole with a splash and grabbed his FAL automatic rifle just as the sky exploded with machine gun tracer, star shells and the bright flashes of mortar explosions. He couldn't believe his eyes. Now, in the light of battle, he could see more British commandos than he could count, advancing quickly across the last few hundred metres of lowland.

His mind, body and emotions reacted with the military instinct that had been driven into him for the past year. He checked his rifle and his ammunition. He would have to make the shots count. Those assholes have to be crazy! There was going to be a lot of death tonight. The Argentine marines that were dug in above Carlos had 12.7mm machine guns, and they were very good with them. It was going to be a slaughter.

He stuck his head out of his foxhole and looked at the violent spectacle. The British commandos were continuing their advance in a dead run towards the base of the hill and firing their weapons wildly. The Argentine marines were now getting accurate with their heavy machine guns, and Carlos saw several British commandos get blown apart. Artillery fire from behind the British increased and began hitting closer to the Argentine mortar pits and heavy machine-gun positions.

It was all happening very fast, and Carlos was overcome with sensory overload. He crouched down in his wet hole and covered his ears with his hands. The bright flash of mortar explosions momentarily blinded him and heavy machine-gun fire echoed in his ears. The smell and taste of sulphurous gunpowder filled every breath, and raw fear took hold of him.

He tried to calm himself. It was time to react. He thought of his Marcela, and the baby that was coming. He was going to be a father!

He took hold of his rifle and stood up, surprising two commandos who were coming up the steep slope not five metres from him. He saw their eyes go wide before he opened fire, and his bullets tore through both of their faces. Adrenalin pumped through his veins, driving his actions and reactions. There was no time to be horrified.

He saw a large group of commandos advancing very quickly, thirty meters to his right and a bit uphill, where his platoon was based. He opened fire with a quick burst and took off one man's arm and knocked two down. The other commandos instantly evaporated into the rocky crags.

Carlos climbed out of his foxhole and ran up the rocky slope, slipping and falling, until he reached the cover of a steep cliff. A loud explosion sounded behind him. The concussion knocked him solidly against the cliff wall and blasted his back with fractured rock. A mortar had made a direct hit on his foxhole.

There was no time to think. The commandos had materialized from the crags, and it seemed there were ten times more of them than before. Carlos could see machine gun fire tearing them apart from only twenty metres away, but there were too many British. They overwhelmed the platoon base.

Carlos ran towards the fight, firing his weapon from his waist. He dropped behind a large white rock and reloaded. He could feel a sharp pain in the base of his neck and found a sharp rock embedded into the vertebrae there. It had passed through three layers of clothes, stopping only when it hit bone.

He crouched low and advanced again. The battle was at close quarters, with machine-gun tracer electrifying the air and grenades exploding. Carlos saw his commander, Second Lieutenant Baldini, fearlessly taking over a knocked out heavy machine gun and killing as many British commandos as he could. But he was totally surrounded and wouldn't be able to last long. Carlos came within ten metres of Baldini, and dropped down behind a rock and opened fire on the three commandos who were pinning Baldini down. All three dropped to the ground screaming, their blood spurting in all directions.

Another group of commandos materialized from a crag and opened fire on Carlos. He crouched down behind the rock just as a bullet knocked his helmet off. He quickly reloaded as Baldini covered him, spraying the rocks with heavy machine gun fire. When Carlos looked around the rock, ready to shoot, he heard Baldini gasp. He turned just in time to see his commander drop his machine gun and fall, face first, downhill into a rock slide.

When Carlos turned back to face the enemy, he found he was completely surrounded. He had to surrender, or die. He wanted to live. He wanted to see his child.

He dropped his rifle and stood up, raising his hands above his head.

Suddenly a commando rose up from a rock right in front of him. He drove the bayonet attached to his weapon forcefully and directly into Carlos's heart.

The world stopped.

The fighting stopped.
Everything went silent.
Carlos could see light.
And, out of the light, he saw his Marcela. She was smiling, with her entire, wonderful face, and she was holding a beautiful baby girl.
With his last breath, Carlos reached out to them.

———

Leonard felt terrible. "I'm sorry, Marcela."

"*Si, yo tambien.*"

"Are you from Buenos Aires? Does your family live here?"

"I have lived here and in El Bolsón, in the southern Andes, northern Patagonia. I was raised by my grandfather there. My parents, well, that's another thing to be sorry about."

Leonard shook his head. "Man, I'm hitting them all."

Marcela smiled, and suddenly she looked like the most beautiful woman Leonard had ever seen. "Argentina is a great country with great people," she said, "but it is also a country simmering with dark secrets, a guilty conscience and deep pain."

"That sounds like Canada and its relations with its Native people."

"I don't know much about that," Marcela said.

Leonard didn't usually reveal much about himself to others, particularly with non-Natives, particularly women and particularly somebody he hardly knew. But he felt that he already owed a piece of himself, a piece of his pain, to Marcela.

———

March 23, 1966
Mary Lake Residential School
British Columbia, Canada

Lenny kept his body low. He moved fast and stayed in the shadows. He had one six-foot wire fence to climb, and he did it in two silent motions. With a few quick steps and a roll, he was lying on the ground next to the girls' dormitory. It took him only forty-five seconds from his bed to the wall of the red brick building. He was getting better at this.

He had started sneaking out from his dormitory at night three months after he and his sisters arrived. He found that winter, during a snowstorm, was the best time. The falling snow made it difficult to be seen, it deadened the sound and it covered his tracks quickly. Usually he wore a white bed sheet tied around his neck, like a cape, to camouflage his dark body against the white snow, but it was March now and the only snow that remained was in places the sun's rays couldn't reach. By June, the daylight hours would be so long that he probably would not be able to sneak out at all. He would have to get his sisters out of there very soon.

Lenny understood that it was extremely dangerous to be out of his bed. If he were caught, his punishment would surely involve the thick leather strap, and without a doubt it would be very painful. But he had to locate Rosie and Christine. This place wasn't a school; it was a prison for Indian kids. His father would never have let them go if he'd known the truth. Lenny had already received the leather strap many times from Father Ricardo for "crimes" as trivial as speaking one word in Carrier.

Lenny had learned that it was best to become invisible and keep his mouth shut. He conformed to the rigid schedule of getting up every morning at 6:30, mass at 7:00, breakfast at 8:00, class at 9:00, lunch at 12:00, class at 1:00, chores at 4:00, supper at 6:00 and back in bed by 9:00. He didn't find the school work particularly difficult, and, except for reading, which he enjoyed, he just found it to be useless information. He also didn't mind doing the chores, mostly cutting and splitting wood, because it got him outside. But, he hated the religious classes, the nuns looking over his shoulder and the priest's glare boring holes into him. The only time he could rebel against them was at prayer time when he just pretended to pray while he imagined himself giving Father Ricardo a good strapping.

He had no idea what his sisters were experiencing, but he knew that they couldn't be having fun. He only saw Rosie or Christine through a fence, and they were difficult to pick out among the other girls. In fact, all the girls looked the same; all with the same page-boy haircut and identical uniforms, blue pants and white shirts, and all their faces expressed either sadness or no emotion at all. There were no happy faces. Even Rosie looked like she was one of the walking dead. She wouldn't look back at him. And Christine appeared angry. Lenny figured that, of all the reasons she might have to be angry, food would be high on her list. The food at the school was meagre and very bad. There were no chocolate chip cookies served here.

It was going to be difficult to find his sisters from outside the buildings. There were two red brick dormitories, each with twenty bunk beds. They had few windows and the girls would all be in bed and under blankets. Lenny would have to get inside, past the nuns, and find Rosie and Christine fast. He was sure the other girls would help him.

But not tonight.

He wasn't ready yet. He had no plan for leaving the school, no idea of where they could go.

He was concentrating on his breathing, mentally preparing for the dash back over the fence and to his bed before the nun's bed check, when silhouettes in a lighted window of the administration building caught his attention. The window belonged to Father Ricardo's office.

For some reason that he could never explain to himself, he did a quick look around and ran the twenty metres to the building as fast as he could. Dropping to the ground, he did a low crawl to the window and stopped to catch his breath. As the sound of his breathing slowed, he could hear something else. At first, he thought it was the whining of one of the cats kept by the school to keep the mice down, but no, it was the sound of a girl softly crying in the priest's office. Lenny looked around to be sure he couldn't be seen, and then slowly rose to his feet. He could see in a corner of the window through a crack in the curtain...

It took him a few seconds to understand what he was seeing and when it finally hit him, it knocked the breath out of him. The priest was behind the girl, forcing her face down on his desk. Lenny couldn't see the girl's face.

The priest had pulled her pants and underwear down to her ankles, and he was running his free hand all over her private parts. He even put his finger inside her!

Lenny dropped to the ground. He had never seen anything like this, and his senses reeled as he tried to get up.

But he wasn't going to look again.

He took a few deep breaths, cleared his head, and bolted for the fence.

——

Leonard summed it up for Marcela. "The objective of these schools was to eliminate Native culture. They called it assimilation. If you spoke your Native tongue, you got a strapping for a word or two. For severe violations, a wooden block was lodged inside your jaws for hours, sometimes days. If you really stepped out of line, you were strapped until you bled. Sometimes with a willow stick on the hands, sometimes with a leather strap. Almost all the children, boys and girls, were abused regularly in every way imaginable. Physically, emotionally, sexually. Children disappeared and died, and all records of them were destroyed. My older sister Rosie was one. Parents drowned themselves in alcohol and died in sorrow. My parents included."

Marcela looked as if she had just heard of her own parents' death. "My God," she trembled.

Leonard continued. "It wasn't that bad for me. I was eleven years old, and I was only there for a year. Some people had to spend many years there, and they suffered way more than I suffered. They are still suffering. On the other hand, I learned over time, after talking to others, not all residential schools were a bad experience.   I only know what a year of it taught me and took from me, and I wouldn't recommend it." He paused when he noticed Marcela wore a sad face. "Although it did bring me to here and now," he continued quickly. "And I am at a sidewalk café in Buenos Aires, with a beautiful Argentine lady and a tiny cup of really strong coffee." He leaned back in his chair and smiled. "Life is good."

Marcela smiled, "Yes, it's not your usual North American cup of coffee." She turned serious again. "Do these schools still exist in Canada?" she asked.

Leonard shook his head. "No, now there are court cases that threaten to bankrupt churches and a culture tampered with and messed up - probably for many generations to come."

"I'm sorry," Marcela said, and she truly appeared to be sorry.

"*Yo tambien*," Leonard replied. "And I'm sorry I depressed you with all that. Usually you can't get two words out of me."

Marcela smiled, but she was still serious. "Thank you," she said.

For a second Leonard and Marcela's eyes locked and touched something deeper. Then, simultaneously, they turned their attention to the sights on the street. The pedestrians were varied and busy: the beautiful ones with their clothes and their bodies, the homeless with their carts and their scowls, the multi-dog walkers, and the Sunday church crowd. None of them paid any attention to Leonard or Marcela.

After a long thoughtful moment, Marcela took a couple of quick sips from her coffee and turned to Leonard. With obvious hesitancy she began speaking. "I was also eleven years old when my life was shattered. My parents disappeared during our military government's Dirty Wars."

———

July 4, 1975
Buenos Aires, Argentina

Marcela stuffed her favourite doll and book into her backpack. She just wished that her mother would tell her what was going on. She wasn't a child anymore; she listened to the adult conversations, even when they spoke in quiet voices. She understood that her father belonged to some kind of group that didn't like the military government. She knew that her father was away most evenings attending meetings with the group. What she didn't understand was why her father didn't come home one night. He just disappeared.

Her mother would only say that he had to go away for awhile. But that's not what her eyes were saying. Marcela could see it in her mother's eyes. She was very worried.

Then, her mother began meeting with other women. Marcela pretended to play with her dolls, but she also listened to their hushed conversations. They spoke of organizing other women, confronting the government and getting answers.

And now, when Marcela arrived home from school, her mother was waiting for her with two packed suitcases. "We're going to visit Abuelo," she announced.

Marcela was stunned. Her grandfather lived in El Bolsón, two thousand kilometres to the southwest, in northern Patagonia, near the Chilean border and a twenty-four-hour bus ride away.

"What about school?" Marcela asked. "And what if Father comes home and we're not here?"

"Don't worry about it!" her mother had snapped. "Let's go."

Buenos Aires' main bus station, Retiro, was a crazy example of organized chaos. Hundreds of people scurried in every direction, while the loudspeakers droned with completely inaudible information. More than twenty buses were lined up in arbitrary parking slots and Marcela and her mother ran with their suitcases from one bus to another, asking other confused travellers the bus's destination. The sixteenth bus turned out to be the one going to El Bolsón. They presented their tickets to the driver, and he crossed their names off the list. After checking their suitcases with the baggage handler, they took their assigned two seats near the back of the bus.

When they were settled with their carry-on things and sat back in their seats, Marcela realized she was hungry, "Do we have anything to eat?" she asked her mother.

He mother closed her eyes and took a breath. "No, we don't."

"That's okay," Marcela said quickly. "I can wait." She didn't want to add to her mother's obvious agitation.

"No, honey, I'm just not thinking right. It's a long trip. I'd better grab some sandwiches and fruit before we go."

Marcela watched her mother hurry off the bus. Outside the bus door, the driver was talking to two men and looking at the passenger list. Her mother stepped off the bus and squeezed past them. As she hurried away to the terminal kiosks, the driver pointed her out to the two men. They quickly followed her into the terminal.

Marcela was frightened. It looked like the men were going after her mother, and they didn't look like nice men. But before she could put her thoughts together, the bus began backing up. Without her mother! Marcela didn't know what to do. She couldn't complain to the driver; he had pointed her mother out to the men. She couldn't complain to the police, because the two men probably were police. After enduring a tornado of thoughts, she decided that she would just stay in her seat, not talk to anybody and pray to the Virgin that her mother would be okay and her grandfather would be there when she got off the bus.

After twenty-four hours of silent crying, not sleeping or eating, thinking a million dark thoughts and reciting every prayer she could think of, Marcela stepped off the bus in El Bolsón a vibrating mess.

And, Abuelo Marcelo was there!

Immediately he swept her up in his arms and gave her a strong hug. "Marcelita, I've missed you!"

He put her down at arm's length and took a good look at her. His face immediately dropped. "What's wrong, mi amor? You look terrible."

He suddenly began looking around franticly. "Where's your mother? Didn't she come with you?"

Marcela fell back into her grandfather's arms and cried.

Her grandfather held her and patted her back. "Pobrecita, don't cry. I'm sure it will be okay."

Marcela could feel her grandfather tense. "I think they took her!" she cried. "She got off the bus and they followed her!"

"Okay, Marcelita, don't worry, we'll find her." He stood up, and for the first time Marcela realized that another man was with them. They both looked very worried to her. She clung to her Abuelo's leg. "I want you to meet a good friend of mine. This is Esteban."

Esteban was a huge man, much bigger than her skinny grandfather, and he had a black moustache. But he smiled and looked like a kind man. Marcela went to him and gave him a hug and a kiss. When he returned her hug, she suddenly felt safe.

Her grandfather's home was a small estancia, secluded and spread out in the lush greenery at the base of the great mysterious mountain, Piltriquitrón. Several very old buildings, constructed of weathered timber and grey stonework, surrounded a circular field of waist-high purple lavender. The huge, jagged mountain loomed in the background. Her mother had told her there was a door to another dimension hidden deep in one of the many inaccessible rocky crags lining the mountain and Marcela never tired of sitting with Abuelo Marcelo, on his porch, sipping maté and searching for the dimensional door.

As soon as she stepped into her grandfather's home, Marcela was pushed straight to the bathroom and ordered to shower and change clothes. She didn't argue. She needed to wash away the last twenty-four hours. She stood under the comforting cascade of warm water for so long that she nearly fell asleep. She was startled when her grandfather knocked on the door.

"Let's go, Sweetheart. The empanadas are getting cold."

She was out of the bathroom in five minutes and sat next to Esteban at the table. She had gobbled down two empanadas before anyone had spoken a word.

"Did you have anything to eat on the bus?" Esteban asked.

She shook her head and kept eating.

"Do you like the empanadas?"

She nodded and kept eating.

When she had eaten as much as she could, her grandfather stood up and put his hand out. "Come on, Marcelita, I'll put you to bed. We can talk tomorrow."

"Good," Marcela agreed. "I can barely keep my eyes open."

She gave Esteban a hug and a kiss and went with her grandfather to her mother's bedroom. He tucked her into the bed and kissed her forehead. "Don't worry, Sweetheart, everything will be fine in the morning." He stood up and turned out the light. "Sleep well."

Marcela knew her grandfather very well and could see the same worried signs on his face and in his eyes that she had seen with her mother. And she knew that everything probably would not be fine in the morning - or ever again.

She waited for several minutes, then slid out of her bed, tip-toed to the door and stuck her head out in the hallway. She could hear Esteban's quiet voice in the dining room, so she slid down the hallway just in her bare feet, far enough to hear what Abuelo and Esteban were saying.

Esteban was speaking. "I'll talk to some people. I'll find out where she is. She'll be okay."

"No, she won't!" Abuelo replied harshly. "They'll kill her just as sure as they killed him! They have no conscience. It's because she was organizing the women." Marcela had never heard her grandfather so angry.

"Maybe not," Esteban said. "Maybe it's a mistake."

There was silence for a few seconds, and Marcela slid a little closer. She could hear her grandfather. He was crying.

———

Leonard sat still with a stunned expression. "Jesus, we make a great pair. Victims of our own country. Did you ever find out what happened to your mother, or your father?"

"Years later, when I turned sixteen, I demanded to know the truth from both Esteban and Abuelo." Marcela took deep a breath. "Two years after my mother was taken from the bus station, her remains were discovered by children building sand castles on the banks of the Rio de la Plata. They suspect she was thrown from a military helicopter into the river. My father was tortured in prison until he died. I won't go into the details."

Leonard didn't know what to say. "I'm sorry."

Marcela needed to focus on something else. "What about your sister, Rosie?"

"I don't know. I've spent my life trying to find out what happened to her. There is just nothing to go on. My uncle went to the school to find out where Rosie had been taken. The residential school records showed that she had been returned to her parents. Of course, that was not the case, because both our mother and father had died the past Christmas, but the priest pleaded ignorance and put off Uncle John's inquiries for quite a few months. Then the priest was caught in the act with another girl, and was quietly and quickly shipped back to Chile, where he held citizenship. And then he disappeared. He was the only link we had to Rosie, the only one who knew what happened to her. Nobody has ever seen him again. Over the years I've followed his tracks, using private investigators. His last tracks ended here in Buenos Aires, over twenty-five years ago. It's the reason I want to check with the embassy here. Maybe dig up some information. Do you know any good private investigators?"

"Well, no, but there's a French-Canadian guy at the Canadian embassy who has been trying to date me since this exchange program started. I'm sure he can help. But it will have to wait until tomorrow, when we can catch him at work."

"This is way beyond your call of duty, Marcela. Don't feel obliged to do it."

"Believe me," Marcela laughed, "I won't be *doing it* with Jean Pierre, but it's the possibility that motivates him. If he can find my home phone number, he can find information on your priest."

Leonard grinned. "I can understand his motivation." Immediately he felt embarrassed.

Marcela smiled. "I think we'd better reel in our driver and pick up Olivia."

———

There were no banks with barred doors near the church where Olivia's choir was practising and the location held no political significance, so the area was free of the sound of the demonstrators' banging pots and pans. In fact, birds could be heard singing in the trees. The old stone church did not look like it had been added to the landscape; rather, it appeared to be part of the bedrock. Ivy grew over the stones like a green tangled net.

Inside, light from the stained glass windows shone on the biblical wall paintings, giving them a luminous aura. Just as Leonard, Marcela and Ernesto entered the church, the choir at the front began to sing. The song was "Noche de Paz", and Olivia was singing lead. Leonard was sure that it was the most beautiful music he had ever heard, this Spanish version of Silent Night. He looked over to Marcela and saw pride radiating from her face. Everything going on outside and inside of Leonard at the moment was new and exotic. A church with reverence. A choir of angels. A woman of pride and beauty. He wanted to remain there forever, but then the song ended, the choir leader said a few words and the angels scattered.

Olivia showed up behind the others and gave the kiss-on-the-cheek greeting to all of them.

"Excelente!" Leonard exclaimed. "That was one of the most beautiful songs I have ever heard."

Olivia's cheeks flushed a couple of shades of red. "Thank you," she said humbly. She looked to her mother. "Where are we going now?" she asked in Spanish.

Marcela replied in English, "We are going to drop Mr. Frank off in La Boca. Then you and I are going to go home so that you can study."

Olivia made a pouting face. "Oh Mother," she sighed in English, "we have all day. We should take Mr. Frank to Esteban's. I'm sure he would love it."

Marcela let out a sarcastic laugh. "I'm sure that you and Pedro would love it," she said, switching back to Spanish. "And that's just the kind of distraction I want you to avoid."

Now the teenager expressed innocence and hurt. "I am not thinking only of myself, Mother. I'm thinking of the culture we can share with Mr. Frank. The tango was practically invented on Esteban's dance floor."

"Oh, it's like a national culture thing?"

"Of course."

Leonard had lost track of the conversation when it moved into Spanish. He looked at Ernesto. "What's going on?" he asked.

The chauffeur shrugged. "It seems that Olivia is overwhelmed by nationalistic pride and wants us to accompany you in a cultural experience. Translated: she wants to see her boyfriend and avoid studying."

"How's she doing?"

"I think you're in for a cultural experience."

Marcela shook her head, *"Pendejos."*

———

Esteban himself was standing outside his tangueria. He was handing a bag of empanadas to a young, shabbily dressed woman. A big man, with grey hair and a grey moustache, he wore a white apron and his sleeves were rolled up. Marcela had said that he was seventy years old, but he looked more like sixty to Leonard.

"Marcelita!" Esteban opened his arms wide. Marcela fell into his bear hug, and then he put her at arm's length, "You honour me! Please come in."

He turned to the young lady he had given the bag of empanadas. "Pedro will bring more tomorrow. Be careful Andrea, there's a lot going on right now." The woman thanked him and walked away quickly with her head down.

"How is your grandfather? The old bastard never comes to the city anymore."

"He likes it quiet, spends a lot of time in church." Marcela indicated the others and spoke in English, "Esteban, this is a colleague from Canada, Leonard Frank."

Leonard quickly put out his hand. "*Mucho gusto*," he blurted out.

Esteban laughed and gave Leonard a hug and a kiss on the cheek. "I like Canadians! Welcome to our country in turmoil." He shrugged his shoulders. "But then, we are always in turmoil." He turned to Olivia. "Young lady, you are getting way too beautiful for your own good. You will have your great-grandfather praying until his knees are worn out."

Olivia laughed. "I think Grandfather's knees already have calluses from mother's teenage years."

Esteban laughed. "Well, women are definitely the topic of many a man's prayers."

"Yes," Marcela added, "and a topic of many a man's confessions."

Esteban replied, "I'm sure you are correct. It's why I, myself, stay pure with women - so that I will not be tempted with sin."

Now Marcela feigned shock. "You are the Original Sin immortalized! There is not a woman within a kilometre of this place, young or old, that has not—"

"Okay," Esteban cut her off. "I'm hearing your grandfather now." He indicated the door with a welcoming sweep of his arm and switched to English. "Please, come in and enjoy some tango. The music is not live, but I have some dancers practising who are beautiful to watch."

Olivia was already through the door by the time Leonard said, "I'd love to see them."

The tangueria was small and lit up and, this early in the day, not very busy. Of its ten tables, eight were vacant. The two remaining tables had been pulled together to accommodate six smiling, camera-clutching Japanese tourists. Tango music set the atmosphere, as a formally dressed-in-black couple filled the small dance floor with their fluid and intricate movements. Their serious expressions, and an occasional naked leg, added a passionate and dramatic effect. The Japanese showed their appreciation with non-stop camera flashes. Two other dancers were attempting to coax a couple of the Japanese to the dance floor, unsuccessfully.

Esteban led the group to a table and pulled out a chair for Marcela. "I'll get Pedro to serve you," he said. "Please excuse me, as I have some empanadas to attend to. Enjoy the dancers, and please feel free to tango." He turned to Leonard. "You know that Marcelita and Olivia are very accomplished with the tango?"

"No," Leonard replied, "they never mentioned it."

Esteban winked at Leonard. "Let her teach you. You'll be a changed man."

Marcela pretended she wasn't listening. Leonard smiled. "I think I'm already a changed man."

Pedro appeared at the table almost as soon as Esteban left. He was a tall, lean twenty-year-old, with soft angular features that made his face appear younger than his body. He wore black pants, black shoes, black shirt and his black hair was tied back into a little black pony-tail. After passing around the menus, he stood next to Olivia like a humble servant. Olivia bit her lip in order not to laugh.

Marcela shook her head in mock disgust and waved them off. "Go!" she commanded. Pedro and Olivia smiled broadly and slipped away, hand in hand.

Leonard watched the young couple walk to the dance floor, face each other, smile, formally place their hands in dance position, and fix their expression, then glide into a seemingly complicated and passionate dance of love. Leonard felt a little uncomfortable watching the young girl do this dance with an older boy, with her mother at the same table. Marcela, was so lost in pride though, watching her daughter move so perfectly, that Leonard began to enjoy the dance, feeling honoured to experience the Argentine culture so closely. He became lost in the passion Pedro and Olivia were expressing so openly. Suddenly he felt a hand on his shoulder and looked up to see Marcela nodding towards the dance floor. "You might as well come out and let me show you some basics, or Esteban will drive you and me crazy and Olivia will jump in for sure."

Leonard grimaced. "Marcela, I'm sorry, but I don't dance."

"Okay," she said, "but you tell Esteban."

Her hand was still on his shoulder. It felt to Leonard as though an electric current was passing directly from her hand, through his shoulder, to his heart. He just looked at her, he couldn't speak. He felt like a total idiot. She smiled sympathetically, and he felt even more stupid.

Suddenly, Esteban was standing at the table. "Marcelita, why aren't you being a good Argentine host and teaching this handsome Canadian the art of the tango?"

CHAPTER FOUR

Christine took the photograph off Leonard's dresser and sat down on his bed while staring into it. It was difficult to look at the picture and see anything but the priest. She felt so much contempt for Ricardo, for how he had destroyed their family. He had taken away Rosie and killed their mother and father. This would be hard to forgive in any religion. Christine was working on her healing, but she had to admit she just wanted to take the priest by the balls, rip his heart out and stick it down his throat.

It didn't surprise her that the image of the priest would stir more emotion in her than the image of her missing older sister. Years ago, after much counselling, she discovered that she had replaced the helplessness and the sadness of Rosie's disappearance with anger and contempt for Father Ricardo. Leonard had taken care of the actual searching for both Rosie and the priest. He had worked fires since he was a teenager and had no bad habits - no drugs, no drinking, and every extra penny he had went to private investigators and researchers and to tracking down leads. Nothing ever came of any of this effort, except that it was likely that Ricardo had taken a plane from Chile to Buenos Aires one day many years ago.

Christine ran her finger across the image of Rosie. She looked so young and pretty, so innocent and hopeful. Even with the stupid page-boy haircut. And she had had such beautiful long hair the day before.

But then, many things were different the day before.

After that day, she never spoke with Rosie again. They were separated the first night - girls under thirteen from girls older than thirteen. A few days later, when Christine caught a glimpse of Rosie, she could see that her usual vibrant brown eyes had turned black and vacant. It was as if she had become a zombie.

Christine missed her sister every day.

It was the roadblock to her heart and soul. Neither she, nor Leonard, could sustain a relationship with a person of the opposite sex for more than a few months. Leonard was a quiet, unemotional, wooden Indian. All his girl-friends were white, and none stuck around for very long. Leonard was not a real fun and engaging guy, although he did have a certain wit that got him in good with a few women. Christine, on the other hand, was way too much fun and too engaging to have only one boyfriend for more than a weekend. The only consistent relationship in Christine and Leonard's lives was the one with each other. Christine always missed Leonard when he was gone, and worried about him when he was on wildfires. She hoped that he would phone, and knew that he would, he always phoned. He missed her just as much, and felt responsible for her.

Christine looked deep into Lenny's expression in the photograph. His almond-shaped eyes were narrowed even more than usual, and she could see that his jaw was tensed. He held his chest out, and stood with his fists clenched defiantly. It was a look he had displayed for her many times, when he wanted to hit her for one of the many things that she had done purposely to piss him off.

——

July 15, 1966
Mary Lake Residential School
British Columbia, Canada

Christine couldn't sleep, even though it had been hours since Sister Anna had turned the lights off. She pulled the woollen blanket over her head and cried softly. She cried only when she was alone. Or when the strapping hurt too much.

She cursed her father for letting the priest and the Mountie take them. At least her mother had tried to stop them. She relived and reconstructed the moment a hundred times, and it usually ended with her hitting the Mountie in the balls with the steel fire poker and then shoving the pointed end into Father Ricardo's eyeball. She figured that since she was just a nine-year-old girl, smaller and weaker, it was best to go for the eyes. One time, when her father had killed a moose, she had stuck a stick in its eyeball to see what would happen. She came to the conclusion that it would probably distract anybody, of any size, for quite awhile and it was easy to do. You just had to have good aim.

Christine did realize that she was kind of a troublemaker, but she didn't think she misbehaved enough to be taken from home and disciplined to this extreme. And why would their father have let them take Rosie? She never did anything wrong. And Lenny should be out in the bush with their father, learning how to be a hunting guide, not in this stupid jail learning how to pray. None of them deserved to be here. This is how people who did really awful things should be treated.

She hated everything.

The food was terrible, but there was never very much to suffer through anyway. She had got her first strapping for telling the nuns that they should pray for a good cook.

She hated class time. It was more difficult for her than for the other girls, and she had received the willow switch across the back of her hands several times for not getting her work finished.

She hated the religious studies classes and praying to their stupid God. She had gotten the leather strap once for asking why their God was such an asshole. They left scars that time.

And she hated doing chores. She usually got stuck with sewing, which she could do all right - her mother had taught her to sew moose hide slippers - she just didn't like to do it.

Again, hands out and the willow switch.

Finally Christine cried herself out, and was almost asleep when she heard something going on quietly at the end of the row of bunk beds. It was probably the priest again. She had lain awake before and seen him come in the darkness and go to a girl's bed. She asked the girl the next day if the priest was bothering her. Crying, the girl replied, "He touched me all over." Since then, Christine had kept a butter knife, stolen from the cafeteria, under her mattress. If the son of a bitch tried to touch her, he was going to have some serious eyeball problems.

She slipped the blanket off her head and listened carefully. She could hear girls whispering. In the darkness, she could see someone coming straight to her.

She fumbled while trying frantically to get her knife.

"Christine," a voice whispered. "Where are you?"

She sat up in her bed. "Lenny? Is that you?"

And suddenly, her brother appeared right in front of her.

She put her arms around him and held him as tight as she could. She was never going to let him go.

"Let's go," he whispered. "We're getting out of here."

Christine jumped out of her bed and started to dress. "We have to get Rosie," she said as she put on her shoes. "She's in the big girls' dormitory."

"No," Lenny said. "She's not here."

"What do you mean?"

"Father Ricardo took her somewhere. I saw them drive away."

"Where did he - "

Lenny cut her off. "Let's go! We have to get out of here before light."

"I don't want to leave Rosie."

"I told you, she's gone and she's not coming back."

"How do you know?"

"I'll tell you later. Now, follow me exactly."

Lenny took off in a low crouch, and Christine followed him out the side door of the dormitory. It was a warm night and the summer sun was already beginning to peek over the eastern horizon. Christine took a deep breath and inhaled the outdoors. She could smell the grass in the yard and the boreal forest a mile away. She could smell freedom.

Lenny silently gave her arm a tug and they took off running across the yard, climbed over two fences and disappeared into the bush. She had to run as fast as she could to keep up with her brother. She kept herself going by reminding herself what would happen if the priest caught them. They kept running, straight into the forest and away from the road.

Lenny seemed to know where he was going. After nearly any hour dodging of pine trees, hurdling deadfall and sliding down steep banks they came to a small creek, jumped in and ran upstream. They followed the flow of water to a small canyon, where the stream turned into a trickle coming out of the ground. Lenny turned at a rock outcropping and straight into a thick stand of black spruce trees.

Christine couldn't go any further. Running in the water had exhausted her. "Lenny, I have to stop."

Lenny didn't stop.

"Lenny!" she yelled. "I can't go on anymore."

He finally stopped, and she caught up with him. He was standing in front of a very old and small log cabin.

"I found this once when we were getting firewood," he said. "I'm the only one who knows about it."

Christine sat down on the ground and tried to catch her breath. "What are we going to do?"

"I've been planning this for a long time. I have snare wire, matches and a knife. We'll stay here for as long as we can. They'll be looking for us at home. We can't go back there right now."

"We can't go home? Then where will we go?" Christine looked around. It was a dark place, surrounded by black spruce, thick with branches down to the ground that only a few rays of morning sunlight could penetrate. She could smell and feel the musky dampness. Mosquitoes were beginning to come alive and rise out of the ferns and spongy moss.

"I have a couple of ideas," Lenny said.

"How are we going to get anywhere?"

Lenny put his hands on his hips and looked down at her sternly. "When are you going to stop whining and complaining?"

"But we don't have anything," Christine complained.

"I just told you," he said. "I have snare wire, matches and a knife."

"Oh, right," she sighed. "And we have this lovely cabin. We're rich."

"You go check out the cabin and clean it up," Lenny ordered. "I'm going set some snares and see if any berries are ready yet. Maybe there's a place to put a fish trap."

"Maybe you should go clean the cabin, and I'll go set snares and eat berries."

Lenny turned and walked away, quickly disappearing into the trees.

Christine swore under her breath and struggled to her feet. The cabin was tiny, dirty and completely rundown. Inside there was just enough room for the furnishings: a table, one chair, a metal bed frame and a wood stove. The roof of the cabin, dirt and moss laid over spruce poles, had succeeded in keeping the inside fairly dry. There was one four-pane window with the two bottom panes broken, and the door wouldn't close all the way. The floor was made of uneven, hand-sawn boards like Christine had watched her father make. In one corner rested a pile of some kind of animal shit. Christine guessed it was a wolverine.

The things that needed to be done to make the place good for the night were obvious. Christine went outside, tore off a big handful of leafy branches from a willow and went back in the cabin. She swept the shelves and table free of spider webs, and used the branches to sweep the floor. The wolverine shit took a little extra effort. Then, she went out again and picked the thickest moss she could find, and an armful of spruce boughs, to lay on the bed spring as a mattress. She gathered wood for the stove, to cook whatever Lenny could catch. She used some rags she had swept off a shelf to cover the broken window panes and keep out the mosquitoes. Then she hammered a floor board down with a rock so that the door would close.

When she decided that the inside of the cabin was habitable, Christine went outside to look for anything she could use. It was going to be a hot July day. She noticed some big, puffy clouds starting to form and knew, from spending most of her ten years outdoors, that with this heat and clouds building higher, they could expect afternoon thunderstorms. It was a good thing they had the cabin for shelter.

Christine found an old blue-enamel cooking pot, two whisky bottles and a rusted cast-iron frying pan buried in the moss near the cabin. Gathering them up, she walked back the way they had come, until she reached the creek and found a small sink-size pool in the stream to wash the utensils. Starting with the cooking pot, she grabbed a handful of sand and scrubbed the dirt and moss from the metal surface. Once she had cleaned the cooking pot down to the rust, she decided they could probably eat off it and survive.

Beginning to wash the frying pan, she noticed a movement on the ground near the trees. She looked closer and saw that it was a grouse. Then she saw another grouse, and another. Four plump chickens on the ground.

She didn't hesitate. Christine had killed a few grouse in the past by throwing rocks, but now she gripped the handle of the frying pan and moved fast. She was on them before they could get off the ground. Soon she had killed three, hitting the first two on the head before they could get their wings operating and the third as it was leaving the ground.

This was becoming a good day. She was out of that stupid jail, she was with her brother, they had a cabin and she had just killed a feast for supper! Her mood was getting brighter.

But she knew that she couldn't be really happy. Rosie should have been cooking these grouse tonight. Christine was confused about why her sister wasn't with them. Lenny hadn't explained, and he seemed to avoid talking about Rosie.

For the first time in what would be thousands of times, Christine found that no matter how great the universe happened to be at the moment, there was a black hole inside her. It created a whirlpool strong enough to suck every bright star of happiness into oblivion.

———

Christine put the photograph back in its place on the dresser. She decided that she didn't like old photos. She also decided that she wasn't going to sleep in Leonard's room while he was gone. She'd sleep on the couch and let the television distract her.

The phone rang suddenly and startled her. She laughed at herself for being so jumpy and answered, "Hello, Leonard Frank's House of Horrors."

"Hey Sis."

"Lenny! Hey Bro, how are you? Where are you? Have you paid for sex yet?"

"I'm fine. I'm in Buenos Aires. And, no. How about you?"

"Well, yes I paid for sex last night."

"Great. How's everything else going?"

"You've only been gone a couple of days, so I haven't really had time to fuck anything up."

"Okay, I'll give you some more time. Everything is going good here. It's summertime, kind of hot and humid. My liaison speaks English and she has set me up—"

"She?" Christine interrupted.

"Yes, she has set me up in a hotel and got me orientated, so right now I'm just wandering around taking pictures, because it's Sunday. And it turns out she has some guy at the Canadian embassy chasing her, someone we might be able get to help us look for Ricardo."

"We? Us? She? You've only been there twenty-four hours! Maybe you won't have to pay for sex. Please, Lenny, for me, use a condom."

"Jesus, Christine, it's not like that. Her name is Marcela and she has a daughter, Olivia. And that's all you get. I'll call you again tomorrow night, around five your time."

"Do you have a contact number there? Maybe the number of the *señorita's* bedside phone? Did you say she was a single mother?"

She wrote down the numbers of Ernesto's cell and Marcela's home phone. "But call me for sure tomorrow. I'll be here waiting."

"Don't worry. You know I always call."

———

Leonard hung up the phone and left the cubicle. He paid for his call at the counter and then went out on the sidewalk. He could hear demonstrators banging pots and pans around the corner and he decided to investigate and get some pictures. He didn't have to walk far. A group of about fifty demonstrators carrying sticks and with bandanas covering their faces was moving along the street and causing havoc. This wasn't the usual pots-and-pans racket by the neighbourhood ladies, but the windows and protective screens of the banks being smashed by a younger, more aggressive group. They attacked a bank machine with iron pipes and destroyed it. There was no money in it. They moved on, spray-painting slogans on walls and breaking windows. Looters came from behind, seeing the opportunity and using the broken windows as doors.

Leonard snapped a few pictures, but the demonstrators were moving too close and he decided to retreat. No need to get in the middle of this group. But suddenly a black van pulled out from a side street, its doors flew open and four police officers dressed in black, with bullet-proof vests, batons and guns jumped out among the demonstrators. They came out with their batons swinging. People in the crowd screamed, and soon they scattered in all directions.

Three bandana-masked demonstrators were now running down the street towards Leonard. Without thinking, he put up his camera to get a picture. The lens was zoomed in beyond the fleeing demonstrators and held the in-focus image of a helmeted policeman pointing a rifle directly at him. The very next second Leonard saw a puff of smoke from the barrel of the rifle, just as a rubber bullet slammed into his forehead.

———

Andrea was running as fast as she could. She was scared to death, so frightened that she was even ahead of Salvador. She heard the shot, and she heard the rubber bullet pass by her ear. She also just happened to notice the man with the blue leaf on his shirt when the rubber bullet violently knocked his head back. It was a man in the group that had approached Esteban earlier in the day, when he gave her the empanadas.

By the time she got to the injured man, a street kid had taken his camera, wallet and passport. Andrea had no time to chase the boy, and probably would have never caught him anyway.

A minivan pulled up beside her. The driver wore a bandana. Andrea went for the unconscious man and yelled to Salvador, "Help me get him into the van! I'll explain later!"

Salvador was not happy, but there was no time to argue. They threw the limp body into the van and disappeared into the maze of Buenos Aires streets.

CHAPTER FIVE

Day Three
December 20, 2001

Marcela rolled over in her bed and looked at the clock. 6:59. Her sleepy eyes remained fixed on the red digital numbers until they turned to 7:00. Then she smiled and curled back under the covers. She didn't have to get up early for work. She was an international liaison now; she scheduled her own time.

It seemed like she had just closed her eyes when the phone rang. She looked at the clock. 9:48. Her hand finally found the phone. "Hello."

"It's Ernesto. Are you awake?"

"No."

"Well, I'm at the Chief's hotel, and he hasn't been back here since we picked him up yesterday."

"What? He's not in his room?"

"Oh wait, I didn't check his room." Ernesto's sarcasm was evident. "No, he's not in his room. Or anywhere near here. I've spoken to the maid and everyone else."

"Shit!" Marcela, still half asleep, had trouble wrapping her mind around the possibilities.

"It could be good," Ernesto went on. "Maybe he hooked up with a sweet Buenos Aires lady." Then he changed his tone. "Or it could be bad."

"What are you talking about?" Marcela sat up in bed.

"Do you live in a bubble? People were shot last night by the police. I'm not sure exactly what happened, but President Del la Rua might resign. There's a lot of chaos on the street. I came down here early to make sure Leonard was okay."

Marcela tried to shake some sense into her head. "Okay," she said finally, "I have to take a shower and wake up. Come over here and we'll figure this out."

Marcela hung up the phone and went straight to the shower. When she came out of the bathroom, awake and dressed, Olivia and Ernesto were sitting at the table staring at the television, sipping *maté*. "Have you seen this, Mother?" Olivia asked. "This is crazy."

"No. What's going on?" Marcela sat down with them to watch the news. Seeing the mayhem on the streets and around government buildings and banks, she muttered, "I hope he wasn't caught up in this."

"Yes," Ernesto said, "Diego wouldn't like that."

"To hell with Diego," Marcela shot back. "I'm worried about Leonard."

"We need a plan," Olivia said. "We need to get out there and look." She looked at her mother, "Would he contact your office? Should you call Diego?"

Marcela shook her head. "No, Ernesto gave him one of his cards with his cell number, and I wrote our number here on the back. I told him to phone me if there were any problems. And it's a little early to alert Diego. I think he has enough on his plate with the government collapsing."

Olivia shrugged. "So, what's the plan?"

"Ernesto and I will get out there and look around," Marcela responded. "You will stay here to answer the phone, if he calls, and study."

"Mother," Olivia pleaded, "I don't need to study, I know the material. And I want to see what's happening out there!"

"I want someone to be here if he calls," Marcela said. More firmly, she stated: "And I want you to study."

—

Andrea had never been in a situation when she was forced to deal with the sick or injured and she had no idea what to do. In her twenty year history there were no siblings or children of her own who depended on her for care. She was born in this house to a wretched woman who could scarcely manage to keep herself alive and, in fact, died from tuberculosis when Andrea was eight years-old. From that point on, she was forced to survive on her own and she grew up in the barrio; filthy and hungry, begging for food everyday. At the age of sixteen, after she had mentally prepared herself for the graduation from panhandling to prostitution, she met Esteban Lopez. Esteban changed her life. He supplied her with all that she needed to live and only asked that she let other people stay in her house about two nights a month. It was a good arrangement and it saved her from becoming a whore.

The injured man had been unconscious all night, but now he opened his eyes slightly and she had no idea what to do. His pupils were milky, and she didn't think he was conscious. She didn't want to alert the two men in the kitchen who were watching the small television. Salvador and Ángel were not the typical anti-government activists referred to her by Esteban; in fact they were not sent by Esteban, but by a woman who had stayed in her house a few months earlier. The people Esteban sent were good people, political activists who were more academic and philosophical than violent; but Salvador, the leader of these two, was just plain crazy. And Ángel was a mindless follower, someone who seemed to enjoy breaking every window on the street with a steel pipe.

They had showed up at her house needing a place to stay for a couple of days, and gave her instructions not to tell anybody that they were there. Salvador talked Andrea into getting them in with some local radicals. The next thing she knew, rather than inciting a takeover of the congress building, as she thought they would do, they were breaking windows, doors and bank machines and encouraging the looters.

When she explained to Salvador that she had to bring in the injured man because he was a friend of Esteban Lopez, Salvador instantly became violently angry. He asked a few questions about Esteban's age and appearance and then said that he knew Esteban from back in the Dirty Wars of the seventies - Esteban had been a prison guard then, was probably a government informant now and, most likely, so was this injured man.

Andrea had wanted to tell Esteban that the infamous Salvador Juárez was staying at her house when she had seen him yesterday at his tango bar, but then his friends showed up and he became distracted. She wished now that she had told him.

Salvador came to the door. His appearance reminded Andrea of what Ché would have looked like if he had lived longer: tall and lean, with a scruffy, greying beard and intense brown eyes. An old scar on the right side of his face gave him a permanent angry expression.

"Fuck him." He said it as if it were an order. "The government is falling. You should come and watch it. The president has resigned, we've burnt the Ministry of Economy office and the police have killed more than twenty people. We couldn't have wished for more."

Andrea wasn't impressed. "His eyes are open, but I don't think he's conscious," she said, looking down at the injured man. His forehead looked very bad, bruised, cut and swollen. His eyes were slightly open, bloodshot and filmy.

Salvador stepped up to the bed and peered into the man's eyes. Without warning, the man suddenly reached out and grabbed Salvador's throat. Salvador slammed his fist against the man's black-and-blue forehead.

Andrea jumped up. "You didn't have to do that!"

"Now his eyes are closed," Salvador said calmly and began going through the man's pockets. "And now you can get us something to eat."

"Some kid already took everything from his pockets as soon as he was shot. This man needs to go to the hospital!"

Salvador glared at her. "He's going somewhere, but not to the hospital." He pulled a business card from the man's back pocket and inspected both sides of it. "He's got something to do with the government, and he was at the demonstration. The bullet that hit him was meant for us. The fact that he is associated with Esteban Lopez makes me even more suspicious of him."

Andrea snatched the business card from him and read: *Ernesto de Salvo, Government Chauffer.* "This card doesn't mean anything," she said and tossed it back at him.

"It might not mean much to you," Salvador said, "but it means a lot to the fate of your friend." He turned and walked out of the room.

Andrea slammed the door behind him. She returned to tending to the unconscious man. He was in bad shape; his forehead was lacerated and swollen, and very ugly-looking. She put a damp towel on his wound and lavender oil on his temples. Despite his facial injuries he was a handsome man with strong features, probably in his forties. His eyes looked Asian.

She could hear the television blaring and the men talking in the kitchen. She went to the door and put her ear close to listen.

Ángel was pacing the floor and talking nervously. "I don't like it - the way he looks, how he's dressed, a government card, the connection to a prison guard who you know from the seventies. We should get the fuck out of here."

"Calm down," Salvador ordered him. "We need to be here right now, in Buenos Aires. We'll just get rid of the guy. He's half dead already."

Ángel didn't calm down. "I don't trust the girl either. She picked him up."

"Don't worry about her," Salvador replied. "We'll take care of that problem also."

Andrea had heard enough. She stood up straight and took a breath. Either she had to get these assholes out of her house or she herself had to get out with the injured man. She opened the door and walked out of the room, into the kitchen.

"I have to get him to a doctor," she stated firmly. "Call me a taxi on your cell phone."

Salvador smiled. "No," he said. "I'm afraid I can't call a taxi."

Andrea wasn't smiling, "Why not?"

"Because that guy isn't going anywhere for a while. He saw me, and the police have my picture posted everywhere."

"He didn't see you. He is totally out of it. He doesn't even know who *he* is! Let me get him out of here *before* he wakes up and sees you, or worse, before he dies."

"Let him die," Salvador responded. "We have more important things to deal with, and he's getting in the way."

The door buzzer sounded and Andrea, nearest to the door, opened it. Esteban's nephew, Pedro, appeared holding a bag of empanadas. "Hello, Pedro," she greeted him nervously. "More empanadas?"

Pedro didn't answer right away. He seemed to be looking past Andrea. Suddenly, Salvador was at the door and snatched the bag from Pedro.

"Now get out of here!" he growled and slammed the door shut. Turning to Andrea, with rattlesnake speed, he grabbed her by the throat and put his mouth to her ear. "Don't ever open that door again without knowing who's there," he half-whispered, half-spit into her ear, "or I will cut your hands off."

———

Leonard could barely see her. The air was thick with fog. Rosie was in the car, looking back at him through the rear window. He started to wave wildly, but she could not see him. He ran towards the car. But he got no closer to it, nor did it get farther away. He strained to see through the fog. He could make out a girl's face, but it was a blur, it had no features. Was it Rosie? How much he wanted to see her face again. How much he wanted to protect her.

Then the face morphed into a man's face. It was the priest. Lenny reached out to grab him.

Suddenly, Leonard felt a blow to his forehead and excruciating pain. Darkness was setting in again. He fought to stay conscious. He could hear angry voices, too distant to understand and see dark figures, too bleary to recognize. A blast of light from an opened door hit his face and he struggled up on one elbow the see better. But still, he couldn't focus.

One figure suddenly lashed out at the other.

It had to be the priest. He was hurting somebody. Who was he hurting?

Lenny was paralyzed. He felt like a coward. After many strappings, he had become quiet and withdrawn. He was a piece of the furniture, witnessing many sins of the father, many kinds of abuse.

But he never stopped the priest. His sin was that he hadn't killed the priest on that first day.
He prayed for forgiveness.
But he would accept death.
He allowed darkness to return.

——

Olivia sat at the kitchen table, fighting boredom by drawing little hearts and jotting Pedro's name randomly on her note paper. At first she had been angry with her mother for leaving her at home, but ten minutes after they'd left, she had successfully distracted herself with thoughts of Pedro.

The phone rang, and she thought of Leonard. "*Hola*," she answered anxiously.

"Olivia, it's me, Pedro."

"*Amor*! I was just thinking of you!"

"I just had a strange thing happen."

"Are you okay? Where are you?"

"Yes, I'm fine. But I'm making deliveries for my uncle, and I think I just saw the Canadian who was with you and your mother yesterday."

"We're looking for him! Where is he?"

"I just saw him for a second, but I recognized the shirt he was wearing – the one with the blue leaf. He was lying on a bed. He looked sick or something. He had a bandage on his head."

"Tell me where he is and I'll phone my mother, so she can go get him."

"No. I'll explain later, but we can't do that. Can you come down here and meet me? Maybe there's something we can do."

"I'm not supposed to leave."

"Well, I don't know what to do, and I'm kind of worried about him."

"Okay, this is serious. Where do you want to meet?"

"At the supermarket, by Retiro."

"That's not a good part of town."

"That's why I'm worried."

"I'll see you in about twenty minutes."

Olivia hung up the phone and wrote a quick note to her mother: "Had to go. Be back soon. Love you."

———

Marcela and Ernesto sat on a park bench in the Plaza de Mayo. They were facing the Casa Rosada, the presidential palace. Thousands of demonstrators filled the plaza and the streets. Most of them were banging pots and pans and chanting slogans.

"The noise is driving me crazy," Marcela complained. "I'm getting a headache."

Diego nodded. "Me too. It's pretty unlikely that the Chief is going to show up here. Maybe we should phone Diego."

"I don't think so. With all this going on and the economic collapse, he doesn't need to hear that we've lost the Canadian."

"We've contacted all the hospitals and police stations. What do we do?" He shook his head. "The government is bankrupt; we probably won't have jobs tomorrow anyway."

"I'm more worried about the frozen bank accounts and Olivia's university money. I can always get another job, but I can't afford to lose that money. It took me fifteen years to save it."

"And, of course," Ernesto added, "you are worried about him."

"Who?" Marcela asked innocently.

"The Chief. You like him."

She waved him off. "I hardly know him."

Ernesto smiled. "Call it a sixth sense of mine. I instinctively know who is willing to go to bed with who, and you—"

"And you are full of shit," Marcela cut him off. "Let's go get some lunch. And I should check on Olivia."

"I'm sure she's fine. She's not a little girl. Give her some room."

"Oh, now you're a parenting expert?"

"I do have some ideas on the subject."

"Well, I've already heard one too many. Give me your phone. I want to see if Olivia needs anything."

Ernesto handed her the phone. "She probably needs some space. If you don't give it to her now, she's going to go wild when she does get it. Catholic school girls have a reputation, you know."

Fortunately for Ernesto, Marcela wasn't paying any attention to him. She was punching in the numbers for the second time. No answer. It didn't make sense. Olivia wouldn't go against her instructions to stay at home.

She handed Ernesto his phone back. "Let's go," she ordered.

CHAPTER SIX

Detective Mónica Garcia opened the thick, red file on her desk, just as she had opened it hundreds of times before in her ten-year career. The black and white photograph on the first page was more than twenty years old, and it made her feel old. It showed a young Latino man with piercing eyes and a very serious face. From this one worn photograph, anybody could see that Salvador Juárez was a bad guy; in fact, the word *psychopath* would probably come to mind.

And this one photograph was all that anybody would have on which to base a profile. Mónica had never seen a more recent photo. There were people who had seen and talked to him in the last twenty years, and Mónica had seen and talked with a few of them. But they would either not give any specifics or not talk about Salvador at all.

Mónica got the idea. To know Salvador was to fear Salvador.

She thumbed the file quickly; she knew Salvador's basic history. He had first come into the picture as a union strong-arm in the seventies, had got caught in a gutting of the union by the military government and was sent to Rawson Prison. He somehow disappeared during the infamous mass escape in 1972 and had made his way to Allende's socialist Chile, eventually establishing himself in a small cinder-block estancia, in a remote part of Chilean Patagonia, within walking distance of the Argentine border. After two months of being out of prison and several trips to Santiago, he had been able to gather a small band of young and militant Argentinean expatriates who were impressed with his participation at Rawson and were ripe for manipulation. When

Pinochet and the CIA murdered Allende in 1973, Salvador and his band of young thugs disappeared into the rocky Patagonian landscape.

The group first surfaced two years later with a "political" action that involved kidnapping an industrialist's teenage daughter. After the ransom had been paid, the young victim made headlines throughout South America by stating that she was in love with Salvador Juárez and had had consensual sex with him and could very well be carrying his baby. That escapade netted Salvador and his entourage enough financial encouragement to disappear from the radar screen for several years as well as netting the industrialist's daughter a baby girl.

In the early eighties, Juárez ran out of money. He surfaced again, while kidnapping a politician's son. Things didn't go as smoothly this time, and the fourteen-year-old boy was killed, as were two of Juárez's closest comrades. Two days later, Salvador made a bold move and kidnapped a government minister's son. Receiving the ransom quickly, he released the boy. He again disappeared for years, and was presumed to be far away from Argentina, perhaps in Cuba or somewhere in the south of Spain.

Now, once again, he surfaced. Mónica's undercover sources had confirmed a couple of sightings of Juárez and his long-time partner in crime, Ángel Méndez, at recent demonstrations around the Plaza de Mayo. They must have come to Buenos Aires to capitalize on the political and economical chaos.

Mónica had learned to hate Salvador Juárez with a passion. She realized that it might appear to her colleagues that she suffered from a compulsive disorder in regard to capturing Salvador, but she didn't give a shit. She was going to get him this time.

Detective Horacio Cortez, Mónica's partner, shifted his weight in the uncomfortable wooden chair on the other side of her desk. He was a bit too large for the chair - in fact he was a bit too large for just about anything to be comfortable; including his clothes, his car and his apartment. Not fat, just big.

"Are you finding anything in there that you didn't already know?" he asked, with a hint of impatience.

Mónica closed the red file. "No," she said, "and it probably wouldn't help us if I did find something. Nothing in there is current. I was just looking to see if we had his old Buenos Aires connection. We'll just have to be very lucky and find him on the street. "

"We have a lot of eyes out there," Horacio assured her. "All of our undercover units and uniformed patrolmen have the bulletin. We've also spread the word through our informant network that there is a reward. We didn't post it publicly, so that we wouldn't scare him off. He probably thinks we forgot about him."

"He's a murderer," Mónica said. Her face was grim. "I'm not going to forget about him."

The phone rang and Mónica picked it up. "What is it, Maru?"

"There's a person on the line asking about the reward," the desk clerk replied.

"Put him through." Mónica put her hand over the mouthpiece. "This might be something," she said, with more excitement than she usually allowed herself to express. Horacio raised his eyebrows and shifted to the edge of his seat. Mónica moved her hand, "Yes, who am I speaking to?"

"My name is Pepe." The voice was old and a victim of too many cigarettes. "I give you guys information sometimes about what happens around the barrio."

"Tell me what information you have." Mónica made it sound like an order.

"Tell me about the reward," Pepe countered.

———

Olivia arrived at the supermarket and spotted Pedro on the corner. They hurried to touch each other, embraced and kissed.

"This has got to be fast," Olivia said. "If I come back with anything short of Mr. Frank, Mother will kill me and I will never go anywhere again. Why couldn't I call her?"

"The house where I saw Mr. Frank is a place that I regularly deliver empanadas to." Pedro's voice was trembling, enough for Olivia to notice. It didn't matter that he was not macho, she loved him anyway. "A lady named Andrea lives there. Esteban gives her the empanadas for free. Today she opened the door and I just had a second to see Mr.

Frank on a bed, in a back room. Then a man grabbed the bag from me, yelled at me to leave and slammed the door in my face."

Olivia stopped walking and turned to her boyfriend. "My guess is, Andrea is a prostitute and Mr. Frank, who was on a bed, and the impatient man waiting his turn, were her customers." Her voice was matter-of-fact, stating the obvious.

Pedro shook his head. "No, I don't think so. Esteban doesn't support prostitutes, he chases them away from his place, and Andrea is not the prostitute type. She wouldn't get picked."

"What do you know about picking up prostitutes?" Olivia asked. Before Pedro could stumble out an answer, she asked, "What about Mr. Frank?"

"I think he was hurt. He had a towel or something on his head, and he looked like he was unconscious." Pedro was excited and scared. "What should we do?" He pointed to a building not far away. "That's the place."

"First you can calm down," Olivia said with a steady voice. "God, that is a scary-looking house."

"This is a scary neighbourhood. I hate coming here. If I wasn't the nephew of Esteban, I would never survive here."

"Where in this house is Mr. Frank?"

"In the back room."

"Let's go behind it to see if there is a window."

"I don't think so. We don't want to get caught by that man."

"I'll just be cute and plead ignorance."

"I don't think that would work with this guy."

"Come on, we're here now. We have to do something. And we have to do it quickly."

They walked nonchalantly, hand in hand, as if they were mindless teenagers, around the house. Avoiding the front window, they ducked down at the back wall. There was another window.

"I think that's the room Mr. Frank is in," Pedro whispered.

Olivia stood up and peeked in at the corner, straining for a view under the curtain. She could see Mr. Frank lying on a bed. There was a poster of Ché on the wall. Nobody else was in the room. Mr. Frank was definitely injured. A wet cloth lay on his forehead, which looked very swollen, and his eyes had black circles around them.

Olivia suddenly felt a violent pull on the back of her blouse and she fell backwards. The next thing she knew, both she and Pedro were dragged, kicking and fighting, into the house by a man with a shaved head.

The man, bigger than both of them together, threw them to the floor and kicked Pedro in the stomach. Olivia screamed and held onto Pedro as he gasped and coughed for air. A bearded man and a woman came into the room. The woman rushed to help comfort Pedro. Olivia knew she had seen the scruffy woman before, but there was no time to think about it.

"Look what I found," the shaved head said. "Seems our delivery boy is making another delivery."

"Leave them alone." Andrea yelled. "That's Esteban's nephew!"

"Esteban Lopez's nephew!" the other man clapped his hands together. "Were you spying on us for somebody?" He laughed. "And a nice little girl-friend."

"They're my friends," Andrea said firmly. "Esteban Lopez keeps me alive."

The man turned serious. "Well, your friends have a problem right now—" the cell phone on his belt rang - "because many years ago Esteban Lopez nearly cost me my life and he gave me this scar." He pointed to his right temple. "He's not my friend."

He turned his attention to the phone. "Hello …… Are you sure? …. Shit!" He put the phone back on his belt. "Let's go, Ángel. This is a setup. They brought the police."

Ángel produced a gun and was pointing it at Pedro. "Should I shoot—"

"Let's go! Now! Out the back!"

"Fuck!" Ángel removed his finger from the trigger and ran.

Olivia couldn't believe it. Free, that easily? She helped Pedro to his feet.

"You have to get out of here," Andrea said. "They'll kill you!"

"We came for the man in the bedroom," Olivia said. "We have to get him."

She and Pedro ran to the bedroom, where Leonard was still comatose. They quickly propped Leonard up in a sitting position, and then each took an arm and stood him up. Leonard groaned and his eyes fluttered open.

Olivia firmly advised him, "We have to go, Mr. Frank."

They shuffled out the bedroom and headed for the front door. Just as they got there, it was flung open. Four policemen charged into the room, yelling and waving assault weapons. Andrea, put up her hands in surrender. Olivia and Pedro held on to Leonard with their eyes wide open in shock. The policemen threw each one in turn face-first to the floor, and held them there with boots to their backs and guns pointed at their heads.

Olivia, now frantic, was crying. A large man and a woman in plainclothes came into the house as if they owned it. A uniformed policeman met them. "No Salvador, no Ángel."

"Take them in for interrogation," the woman ordered. "Put them in separate cells."

———

Marcela unlocked the door and walked into the apartment. Ernesto was a step behind her. The apartment was dead quiet. "Olivia!" she called out as she walked into the kitchen. She saw the note right away, because she was looking for it.

Ernesto was reading it over her shoulder. "There's not a lot of information here," he observed.

Marcela shoved him away. "At least I know she's okay."

"What do we do now?"

Marcela looked at her watch. It was nearly six o'clock. "All this stress and banging pots has made me tired. I need some peace and quiet for a couple of hours."

"Take a rest," Ernesto responded. "I'm going to check out a few things. Call me when you're ready to go again."

As soon as Ernesto had closed the door, Marcela dropped to her reading chair. What the hell was Olivia thinking? This was not like her. She knew exactly how much information her mother needed to feel comfortable; she knew how much her mother worried. And she knew why her mother worried. She had always been the perfect daughter;

well behaved, good in school and respectful. Marcela knew what could happen to a girl her age. Shit, she had gotten pregnant with Olivia when she was Olivia's age. That thought scared Marcela and caused her to worry even more. She worried about Olivia, she worried about Leonard. She worried about her bank account and she worried about Argentina.

She worried herself to sleep.

———

Pedro sat on the edge of his cot staring at the cell floor. The basement jail was a gloomy place and stank of urine. The corridor between the cells was lighted but the cells were not. He felt the guard staring at him and glanced toward the guard, on the other side of the bars. Smiling, the guard pursed his lips into a kiss and whispered, "Later, pretty boy." Then he turned and strolled down the corridor to Leonard's cell, humming a song.

Pedro's chest ached with emptiness and his legs were numb. He hated himself for being so overwhelmed with fear and anxiety. He wished he could be more macho, as he acted when he danced the tango. More outspoken, less silent. More a leader, less alienated. More like his Uncle Esteban, less like his late father.

Pedro's mother and father were well-known tango singers in the eighties and travelled from town to town performing in small venues. It was said they expressed all the emotion possible in every tango they sang. A head-on car crash on a desolate Patagonian highway killed both of them. They were on their way to Las Grutas to pick up Pedro, who was spending a two-week holiday on the beach with his uncle, Esteban. Pedro was seven years old. He had stayed with his uncle at the tangueria since the crash.

Esteban was the kind of man most men wanted to be and that most women wanted to be with. Handsome, strong, witty, charming and generous, he was a confirmed bachelor. He was also an idealist, often in conflict with the government. Pedro didn't know what the conflicts were; Esteban didn't talk politics with him. Pedro only knew that Esteban had been a prison guard during the Dirty Wars in the seventies and at some point had become a sort of an activist to prosecute the leaders of the government and military for their crimes. There were many meetings in the back room of his tango bar to dig up evidence and locating past officials to prosecute.

Although Esteban was strongly independent and single, he had made an effort to raise Pedro in a fairly structured environment. It helped that all the lady tango dancers took Pedro under their wing and made sure that he got to school, did his homework, completed his chores and attended tango lessons.

Pedro was certain his uncle would find him and get them all out of jail. But still he couldn't control his anxiety. He had a strong feeling that things would get worse before they got better.

———

Leonard was gaining consciousness, but slowly and with difficulty. And it wasn't really consciousness. He still couldn't see anything specific, only dark forms with no definition. He could hear only muffled sounds in the distance. More importantly, he was still so confused that he had no idea where he was or, for that matter, who he was.

He tried to sit up. His head exploded. He persevered and managed to force his body into a sitting position. He made an effort not to burden himself with too many questions. He didn't really need to know much at the moment; it was more important now to be able to sit, see and hear. He put his elbows on his knees, then his face in his hands, and tried to put his headache in the background. After a few minutes of vertigo he managed to open his eyes, but only a little, just a sliver of light hurt.

After a few more minutes, he could look towards the light. It a soft yellow glow overlapped with a blurry grid, much like a window frame with panes. Leonard's mind drifted to the window at the residential school dorm, where he had spent many hours gazing out at the tree line and planning an escape. His planning then had eventually brought him and Christine to the other side of the window. But he was too late for Rosie.

A dark silhouette appeared in front of the yellow glow. Although Leonard couldn't make out the details, the feeling was ominous and dark and he knew Father Ricardo had returned. He could hear the priest's cruel laugh. Then the figure moved away.

Leonard stayed sitting, with his head in his hands. He didn't want to lose that position, but he was enduring a rush of emotions. He felt scared, helpless, mad and sad, all at the same time. He closed his eyes, wanting it all to go away, but spinning and falling sensations overwhelmed him.

—

Olivia could hear the guard making his way down the corridor, from cell to cell. She heard him leave Pedro's cell shuffling his feet and humming, pausing at Leonard's cell, laughing, then shuffling on and humming. Now he arrived at her cell and stopped. She could see that he was a big man, with sweat stains on his shirt and black, wiry hairs sticking out from under his cuffs and collar. He leered at Olivia and fondled his crotch.

"Hey, *chica*," he drooled, "are you feeling bad? I have something here to make you feel good."

Olivia glared at him. "Leave me alone!"

"You just need a man. You've probably never had a real man like me before."

"And I never will," Olivia blurted out. "You're gross and ugly!"

The guard's expression changed and he stopped playing with himself. He took a key from his belt, opened the cell door and walked in.

—

Mónica didn't want to waste any time; she and Horacio were eager to interrogate the four captives they had locked up. They agreed to stay all night, if that's what it took. "We'll start with the young girl," Mónica said as she looked down at the list of names on her desk. "Olivia Cruz. She'll probably give us the most information the quickest."

"Yes," Horacio agreed. "Her boyfriend is more vulnerable. But he would only whimper. The other lady, Andrea, obviously has some experience with the police, so we probably won't get much out of her for a while."

"You'd better get someone to take the injured man to the hospital. Andrea was pretty vocal in letting us know he'd been shot by the police with a rubber bullet. Olivia gave his name as Leonard Frank, a Canadian here on business. I tend to believe both of them. They don't seem like the radical revolutionary type."

"No," Horacio agreed, "but that was definitely a safe house, and Salvador and Ángel definitely just occupied it. And these four were definitely there. There has to be some connection."

Mónica was trying not to show her excitement. She had to think fast and smart and not let this opportunity slip by. "Let's see what that connection is."

"I'll get the guys up front to take Mr. Frank to the hospital emergency and I'll bring Miss Cruz to the interrogation room." Horacio stood to leave. "You may have to get a new hobby," he said with a grin. "I think we're going to catch this guy."

Mónica didn't smile. "He's not my hobby," she said coldly. "He's a cold-blooded killer who has eluded justice for thirty years."

Horacio raised his eyebrows, "Okay," he said. "But what about all the more recent cold-blooded killers on our list?"

"We'll deal with those after we deal with Mister Juárez."

Horacio turned to leave, but Mónica stopped him. "Horacio."

"Yes, Boss?"

"Thank you for agreeing to stay tonight. You know you don't have to."

Horacio smiled. "I wouldn't miss it for the world." He closed the door behind him as he left her office.

Mónica was thankful that he agreed to stay all night. She knew that he had agreed because he realized that catching Salvador meant a lot to her. For him it was just another case to work on. His motivation for becoming a detective was to go after rapists. When he was nineteen, his sister had been raped while she waited for him to pick her up from a dance. She was sixteen at the time.

But for Mónica, Salvador wasn't just another case, not even a person. Salvador was a lifetime goal she had set for herself.

She tried to shake off the frustration of having just missed him. She had come close a couple of times, but this was the closest. She could still smell Salvador in the house. She wasn't feeling much optimism about the four people they were holding - Salvador was too smart to let anyone know where he was going, especially any person in that group. Mónica was sure that he didn't even know where he would go; but she knew he wouldn't leave Buenos Aires. It was a city ripe for crime done on false political pretense, his specialty. She just had to ramp up the pressure and keep the word of reward out on the street. It had worked once; it could work again.

CHAPTER SEVEN

Day Four
December 21, 2001

Marcela was shifting her sleeping position when she suddenly realized that she had fallen asleep in her over-stuffed reading chair. She looked at the clock; it was 1:00 am. Jumping up, she went straight to the bedroom. Olivia wasn't there.

Marcela felt her panic raise. She went to the phone and called Ernesto's cell.

"*Hola*," Ernesto answered. Loud music and nightclub voices filled the background.

Marcela got straight to the point, "Olivia isn't home."

"It's early," Ernesto laughed. "She's probably tangoing the night away."

"Well, can you come and pick me up, so that I can find her and drag her tangoing ass home."

Ernesto knew enough about Marcela to recognize the don't-fuck-with-me-right-now tone of her voice. "I'll be there in ten minutes," he assured her.

———

Olivia stood and backed herself into the jail cell wall. "Get out of here!" she yelled at the guard.

He smiled and unbuttoned his pants. "Now, we can make this easy and you can go down on me," he said, "or you can fight it and I'll fuck you like you've never been fucked before." He opened his pants and exposed his semi-hard penis.

Olivia's mind raced. There was nothing in the cell she could use to defend herself. The guard moved in closer. "How will it be, *chica*? In your mouth, or up your ass?"

Olivia could smell his sweat. She prepared to kick him between the legs as hard as she could. She knew that he would be expecting it, and if she didn't put him on the floor with the first kick, he would hurt her badly.

Someone else was moving silently into the cell behind the guard. Olivia couldn't see his face, but she suspected that things had just got worse; it must be another participant. The guard saw her eyes looking beyond him and turned. The shadow hit the guard with so much force that the guard's head hit the cement wall. Blood exploded from his head at the point of impact. His eyes rolled into his head and he dropped to the floor.

"Are you okay?" the man asked in a friendly tone, as if he hadn't just smashed a man's head to the wall. Olivia recognized him as the large plainclothes policeman who had raided Andrea's house.

Olivia relaxed her kicking foot. "I'll be a lot better if you get me out of here."

The man ignored the bleeding guard on the floor and put out his hand. "Come with me."

"Where?" Olivia asked, suspiciously.

"I'm not going to hurt you," the man said. "My name is Detective Cortez. I'm bringing you to see my boss. She's curious about what you were doing in that house."

Olivia was encouraged that his boss was a she. She pointed to the bleeding guard. "What about him?"

"He's fired."

Olivia took the detective's hand, stepped over the guard, careful not to slip in the blood, and followed Detective Cortez out of the cell. They went through a couple of dark corridors, entering a room with a table and three chairs. A dark mirror, obviously a one-way mirror, was built into the wall.

"Have a seat," Detective Cortez said. "I'll get my boss."

Olivia looked around the small room. Her eyes settled on the mirror. "I guess this is a step above the cell and the perverted guard," she said. "When you said that your boss was curious, you meant that your boss wants to interrogate me."

The detective grinned. "Exactly." Then he left the room.

Olivia sat down, smoothed the wrinkles in her blouse and waved to the mirror. This was something she was good at - appearing to be unaffected. She did it all the time with her mother, her teachers, generally with all authority. She had no idea of why she did it, and no idea why she would do it now, when she was justifiably scared to death, but she knew that she had to keep it up. This thing would be over soon. And soon she would be at home, in bed, crying hysterically.

She had to wait only a few minutes before Detective Cortez returned with his boss - a serious-looking woman, in her mid-thirties, with black shoulder-length hair and a black pant suit. She was the one in charge during the raid. The sombre woman sat down across from Olivia and looked directly into her eyes.

"Olivia, my name is Detective Garcia. I'm here to interrogate you regarding Salvador Juárez and Ángel Méndez." She emphasized *interrogate*.

"I have no idea who they are," Olivia replied.

"They escaped the safe house where we picked you up just before we arrived."

Olivia considered herself a good judge of character and she immediately understood that Mónica was not someone who would tolerate the smartass teenager routine. "All I know about them is that they would have killed us, if you hadn't shown up," she said.   "Did you catch them?"

Mónica ignored the question. "What were you doing there?"

"Pedro and I went there to get Mr. Frank."

"Okay." Mónica's voice sounded tired. "Let's forget the interrogation shit. It's late. Tell me how you got there and what happened while you were there. Don't leave out anything, and I won't have to ask you many questions."

———

Leonard didn't realize he was being helped to his feet until he was standing. His mind was as unclear as his vision. His consciousness was awakening but had stalled at eleven years old. He was being led away by someone he perceived to be Father Ricardo.

Leonard sensed where he was going. He was going to get strapped. He couldn't remember what he had done wrong, but it had to do with speaking Carrier, the language his mother had taught him since birth. He was trying to get used to speaking English and only English at the residential school, but whenever he uttered a single word in Carrier he was strapped black and blue. Sometimes the priest made him hold his hands out, palms down, and hit his knuckles brutally with a willow stick. At other times Leonard had to bend over the priest's desk, pants down, and the leather strap would sear his naked butt. Both punishments left lasting marks on Leonard's body and soul.

The priest led him through cool, dark corridors and upstairs, then outside into the warm night air. Leonard's vision was starting to clear up, even if his mind was not. The priest was putting him in the back of a car. A warm glow of optimism washed over Leonard's anxiety. Maybe the priest would take him where he had taken Rosie.

———

Marcela had to wait longer than ten minutes for Ernesto to arrive, but it takes longer than ten minutes to get anywhere in Buenos Aires. "I hope you haven't been drinking," she said as she got into the car.

"I'm a lover, not a drinker," Ernesto replied. "Where are we going? My guess is Esteban's tangueria."

"You guessed correctly."

Ernesto drove in silence while Marcela tried to unscramble her brain. What was going on with Olivia? It didn't make any sense at all. She had always appeared to be an independent and strong young lady on the outside; but Marcela was her mother, and her mother knew that Olivia was still a vulnerable, young girl on the inside. She would debate any issue, but in the end she would always do what she was told. Always.

They pulled up to Esteban's. Marcela ordered, "Stay close. We won't be here long."

The dance floor and the tables were a lot busier now, in the middle of the night, than early in the day. Several local couples, at all skill levels, were tangoing to a live trio with a lady singer. Ernesto headed for a table of teenage *gringas*. Marcela hoped he would have the sense to warn them that La Boca wasn't a safe district for teenage *gringas* at night.

She found Esteban behind the bar, dressed up in a twenties-style suit and hat.

"Marcela!" He clapped his hands together. "You're becoming a regular customer. Are you looking for a job?" He looked closer. "You look troubled."

"I'm looking for Olivia. Has she been here tonight?"

Esteban's face darkened. "No, I haven't seen her. Would she be involved with demonstrations?"

"No," Marcela waved that notion off. "She isn't political at all. She doesn't even understand what's happening." She looked around the room. "Where's Pedro? Can I talk to him?"

"I don't know where he is. I sent him on deliveries this afternoon, and he hasn't returned. In fact, he hasn't even phoned." Esteban's eyes widened with a realization. "You don't think they could be together, do you?"

"That's my first guess. Any idea where we could find him?"

Esteban thought for a few seconds. "Let me make some calls," he said. "I should be able to narrow it down. Can I get you a drink?"

"I'll get a coffee, you make your calls."

Esteban disappeared and Marcela went behind the bar and fixed her coffee. She knew the tangueria like she knew her apartment. She had worked behind the bar and on the dance floor almost every summer in most of her teenage years. It was where she had met Carlos and, in fact, where Olivia was conceived. Olivia also had worked for Esteban. Olivia and Pedro had practically grown up together in this building. Marcela was surprised that their friendship had blossomed into a romantic relationship rather than a brother-sister one. And now it had perhaps become deeper.

Marcela shook her head. It was inevitable and probably contrived from the start. It definitely had the smell of the sort of stew Abuelo and Esteban would stir up - a pinch of Esteban's romance and a dash of Abuelo's practicability. Marcela was sure, in their minds Olivia and Pedro were already married and running the tangueria. They were just waiting for it to happen.

March 13, 1976
El Bolsón, Argentina

Esteban wrapped his dear friend Marcelo in a bear hug.

"Thank you for doing this," Marcelo said into Esteban's ear.

Esteban stepped back at arm's length. "Brother, I am not doing this for you. There's no need to thank me. I am finally doing something I should have done many years ago. Again, I am thanking you for putting up with me."

"If you had not been with me these last four years…" Marcelo hesitated as he took a breath to hold back his emotion. The bus station was not the place for a tormented man to finally let go. "Thank you, Brother," he said simply. "Call me."

Esteban picked up his bag. "I'll be phoning you every day for your business sense."

Marcelo waved him off. "Don't listen to me - or you'll be back soon, with no money and picking tomatoes."

"Perfect," Esteban laughed. "That life suits me fine."

He turned to get on the bus, then stopped and turned back. He frowned at his friend. "What I find out may not be good."

Marcelo put his arms out. "Can it be worse than not knowing?"

In this case, Esteban thought to himself, with all the horrific tales of electro-torture and rape, it could be worse to know. But he said, "I'll call," and climbed the stairs onto the bus to Buenos Aires.

At the age of forty-seven, Esteban decided that it was time to return to the real world. His father and mother were old and sick in Buenos Aires and could not continue to operate the family-owned tango hall. His father had begged Esteban to come back to the city, take over the business and keep it in the family. His younger sister still lived in Trelew and had no interest in tango, or in the business. His older sister took off with a singer.

Esteban was convinced to return to Buenos Aires only at the urging of his friend Marcelo. Marcelo pushed the most - he had been Esteban's best friend since childhood. Esteban had learned over the years to respect his friend's advice more than his own intuition. They had grown up together on the streets of La Boca in Buenos Aires and had spent most of their time within two city blocks of the tangueria. Marcelo's mother and father operated a small empanada and pizza stand directly across the street.

The two boys couldn't be more different. Esteban was a big, fun-loving jokester who spent more time avoiding work than actually doing it; Marcelo was a tiny kid, a pragmatist who did some kind of work every day of his life. Esteban didn't give serious thought to anything beyond the here and now; Marcelo was a devout Catholic and planned for the future. But they became inseparable and at the age of twelve made a solemn vow that together they would get out of the city as soon as they could.

On January 3, 1946, the day Marcelo turned eighteen, they drove out of Buenos Aires on small motorbikes with backpacks and headed south to Patagonia. For more than two years, they worked, broke down, tangoed and partied their way south along the Atlantic coast, through every beach town and desolate estancia to Tierra del Fuego. Then they headed back up the other side into the southern Andes, along the border with Chile, to Lago Puelo and the small lush valley of El Bolsón.

It was obvious to Marcelo as soon as he set his eyes on the mystical mountain, Piltriquitrón, that he had found his place and was parking his motorbike for the last time. Within a year, he had found a job caretaking a cattle ranch, moved into a beautiful stone house in a lavender field and married the owner's daughter, Olivia. The woman of his dreams. One year later, Olivia died giving birth to their daughter. Marcelo - or what was left of him - named the child after her brave mother and his cherished wife, Olivia.

Although Esteban came to and left El Bolsón regularly, he did not settle anywhere. When he came to El Bolsón, he spent most of his time helping Marcelo to be a parent for the rebellious little Olivia and he made a meagre living dancing and teaching tango wherever there was a demand. He was fond of the saying, "To have more, desire less" and all that he desired was a variety of female companionship, gas for his motorbike and enough food to get through the day. His favourite story was of coming across Ché Guevara on his motorbike while Ché was going the other way on a remote Patagonian trail. They shared maté and talked about motorbikes, road conditions and the girls in Bariloche.

And, for twenty years, throughout the fifties and sixties, that was good. Motorbikes, roads and girls.

Until the seventies.

Four years ago, Esteban had gone to visit his little sister in Trelew and, for the first time in his life, he got a job that had nothing to do with tango or having fun. His sister's boyfriend landed him a position at the Rawson prison.

He had worked for only six months, until the day he heard that the nineteen prisoners who attempted to escape had been taken to the naval base and massacred. His political neutrality ended that day. He knew all nineteen victims and there hadn't been a violent criminal among them. One of the women was even pregnant. Esteban was stunned that the military government was so brazen and vicious. He returned to El Bolsón, far from the heat of political fire.

El Bolsón, as it turned out, had become one of the "in" spots for the upper-middle class to send its revolutionary college-age kids to hang out and avoid the authorities. The kids loved it, as their parents sent money, and they did drugs and had sex. Communal living was becoming common. Esteban got to know the hippie refugees who had settled in the area close to Marcelo's estancia and found that he enjoyed the company of a couple of the more political-minded groups. And they seemed to accept him, even though he was twenty years older than most of them. They liked music, they didn't have real jobs and on a good night Esteban could find himself in bed with a sweet girl half his age. He would even take a hit or two from the joint that perpetually made the rounds at every communal table, even though he didn't care for the high — it ran counter to his gregarious personality.

Then the brutality of the military government reached his dear friend Marcelo and touched his own heart. First, Olivia's husband had disappeared after a government raid on a meeting. Frantic she tried to get some answers about what had happened. Then Olivia herself disappeared. The only good thing for Marcelo was that his granddaughter, Marcelita, made it to him. But now Esteban was as crushed as Marcelo had become. Life in Argentina was getting stupid — and dangerous.

When the letter from Esteban's parents arrived, he was uninterested. He didn't want to return to Buenos Aires, and he didn't want the responsibility of the tango hall. He was content to stay in El Bolsón, to help Marcelo with the estancia and to help with Marcelita.

Then one night around a fire, after several bottles of wine, a skinny girl with dirty-blond hair and a gold tooth looked innocently at Esteban and exhaled a cloud of marijuana smoke. "Why do you take it?" she asked and passed Esteban the joint.

"What do you mean?" Esteban asked and took the joint.

The girl shrugged her boney shoulders. "Don't you have any inclination to stand up against injustice — to do something about it?" Her voice was soft and sweet. "You've seen the injustice with the Trelew Nineteen — you knew them. They were all murdered. Your goddaughter, her husband — disappeared. Likely murdered. You've heard first-hand accounts of the worst kinds of torture. Doesn't it make you want to do something?"

Esteban was caught off guard. He was thinking she might be interesting in bed, and she was asking why he didn't have the balls to do anything about injustice. He took a long hit off the joint. "What can I do?" he asked and exhaled. "I'm not going to bomb anywhere or hurt anyone. I don't believe that works."

"You don't have to," the girl said. "You can do a lot of things to help the movement without killing. The murders need to be brought to justice. You know many innocent people are fugitives. They need help as they move around. You would be good at logistics."

Esteban instantly understood what was going on — pretty girl, sweet voice, wine and marijuana — he was being recruited. He took another hit off the joint and passed it back to the girl. They didn't speak for a moment and Esteban thought about the prospect. When his friend's daughter, his own goddaughter, Olivia, was taken, he secretly cried for hours. But not in front of Marcelo. He had to be positive and strong for Marcelo. And he did harbour guilt from keeping his mouth shut when he should have spoken. Getting involved with logistical help could be a good way to do his part to support the movement and a good way to find out what happened to Marcelita's mother. A good way to change.

"I would consider logistics," Esteban said finally.

The girl smiled and her gold tooth glittered.

Esteban wasn't thinking about her bedroom skills now. He was realizing this was an important moment. He was making a commitment to be committed. He would go to Buenos Aires and take on his responsibility in the family business, he would find out what happened to his friend's daughter and he would fight the good fight.

———

Marcela was finishing her coffee, watching the tango dancers glide across the dance floor and getting impatient when Esteban finally returned. "I've phoned all the places Pedro had to go, but one," he said. "He had been to all of them."

"What about the one you couldn't phone?" Marcela asked.

"There is no phone there," Esteban replied. "We should probably check it out."

"We have a car here."

"Let's go. I'll just get one of the girls to watch things."

"And I'll break Ernesto away from that table of girls."

It took over a half hour, following Esteban's directions, for Ernesto to manoeuvre his way through the city streets to get to the neighbourhood where Pedro was to do his deliveries. Esteban had Ernesto pull over in a dark area of the street.

"This is the place?" Marcela asked. "There's no house here."

"Not exactly," Esteban said. "It's just ahead, but I'll walk from here. In this area, having this type of car pull up to your house is usually not a good thing."

"What kind of place is this house?" Marcela was beginning to worry. "Who lives there?"

"I'll explain later," Esteban said and got out of the car. "I'll only be a few minutes." He disappeared into the darkness.

Ernesto immediately rolled up his window and locked the driver's side door. "Yes," he said sarcastically. "This is where I want to hang out. It's nice here."

"Relax," Marcela said. "He won't be long."

Ernesto turned to her. "Are you relaxed?" he asked.

"No, but I'm not scared. At least it's quiet here."

Suddenly and violently, the two side windows exploded with broken glass. Both Ernesto and Marcela found their heads being pulled back by the hair, and knives at their throat. Their attackers wore bandanas to cover their faces.

The one holding Ernesto spoke. "You don't look like you belong here."

Ernesto's eyes were wide with terror. "You're correct. We don't belong here."

The attacker tightened his grip. "Then why are you here?"

Marcela spoke. "We are waiting for—"

Her captor pulled her hair back. "Shut up, bitch. He was talking to Romeo." He pressed the knife blade to her skin.

Ernesto spoke up, "We're waiting for—"

"Me!" A stern, dark voice sounded from the shadows. Esteban stepped out into the moonlight on the street. Even at the age of seventy-three, his large frame in tango attire with a twenties style suit and hat, he cast a sinister silhouette.

Marcela's attacker immediately let go of her hair. He stood up straight and put his knife at his side. "Esteban!" His voice became submissive. "We had no idea it was you. We have to be careful these days."

"Take the bandanas off," Esteban ordered as he strode to the car, "Apologize to Miss Cruz and our driver."

Both attackers pulled down their bandanas. They were young men, barely twenty. "Sorry," they said simultaneously, looking at the ground.

"Why isn't anybody at the safe house? Where's Andrea?"

Ernesto's attacker spoke. "The house was raided."

"By who?"

"The police. We got Salvador Juárez and his friend out just in time. But they got Andrea, Pedro and two others, a girl and a man."

"Salvador Juárez? What was he doing there? Why didn't anyone tell me about this?" Esteban was angry now.

"It only happened tonight, we thought you knew—"

Esteban cut him off. "And what the hell was Salvador doing there? He's supposed to be in Cuba."

"They showed up at the Plaza de Congesso a couple of –"

"It doesn't matter now," Esteban said impatiently. "Get out of here."

The attackers disappeared into the darkness as quickly as they had arrived. Esteban got into the back seat of the car with Marcela right behind him. "Let's go," he said.

Ernesto was picking the shards of broken glass off his clothes. "Go where?" he asked. "Far away from here, I hope."

Marcela turned in her seat to face Esteban. She was white with fear. "What's going on here, Esteban? Where is Olivia?"

"I don't know," he replied. "But let's find out. Ernesto, take us to the police station, please."

CHAPTER EIGHT

Christine was never known for her patience, and it was starting to show. Aunt Josette had tried to teach and demonstrate patience through Christine's formative years. But Christine didn't get it.

"Patience is a virtue," Auntie had told Christine when she was twelve and wanted to go to a teenager party.

"What's a virtue?" Christine had asked.

"It's a good trait. It's a moral quality in a person."

"How do I get virtue?"

"You learn what virtues there are and practice them whenever you can. I go by the seven heavenly virtues that oppose the seven deadly sins. Patience is one. Chastity is another."

"Maybe you should tell me more about those deadly sins."

It was a good thing Aunt Josette looked at Christine as a challenge and a work in progress, or frustration would have killed her. Aunt Josette did have the virtue of patience and she used it everyday to give Christine the social and academic tools she needed to function in the world.

Christine was wishing now she had learned patience back then. She picked up the phone to check for a dial tone. Leonard always phoned her when he said he would. Sometimes, when he was chasing fires, his call didn't come at the specified time, but this was way overdue. Christine had lots of time to think of reasons why Leonard wouldn't phone this time - the lines down or busy, a prolonged meeting, an unexpected social event, but nothing she could imagine allayed her concern. He had said that he would phone at 5:00 pm and now it was past midnight here in British Columbia, which put it past 5:00 am in Argentina. He couldn't have forgotten to phone, it just wasn't possible.

She went to the kitchen and put on a pot of water for tea. She wished she had a cigarette: this was a good time to start smoking again. She hadn't even thought about it for over a year, probably because life had been good and without stress. Her job for the local newspaper as the First Nations reporter was working well and turning into a career. When she was hired, Christine was sure that she would only be the token Indian - which she was fine with her, as long as she was compensated fairly. She didn't intend to work there long. It was after her story on crystal-meth on the reserve when the editor-in-chief, known throughout the office as the Dragon Lady, had called Christine into her office.

"Your articles are causing attention." She always spoke in a dry monotone. "Attention that we don't necessarily want to attract."

Christine thought that was peculiar. "Isn't it good for a newspaper to attract any kind of attention? More people buy the paper, the circulation increases and more advertisers are standing in line."

"But the demographic that you attract is not the demographic that buys our paper."

"It is now. I've just added another demographic and probably have doubled your circulation. Potential advertisers will notice that. Many of them have already identified this market. Don't you think Indians buy cars and washing machines? I thought you called me in here to give me a raise and my own First Nation section of the paper."

The following week Christine had her own two-page First Nations section and a hundred dollar per week raise. After a year, the newspaper had spread into surrounding First Nation communities, tripled its circulation and doubled its advertising revenue. And the Dragon Lady and Christine had become drinking buddies.

The phone rang. Christine let out a breath. *Finally.* She picked up the phone and didn't waste time with formalities. "Why took you so long? I've been waiting hours for you to call. Don't tell me you're going to call and then not call. I have a life, you know."

"I'm sorry honey. I had a hard time finding your brother's number."

Shit, it was the guy she slept with last weekend. She couldn't remember if his name was Jim or John. "Oh, it's you, "she said. "I told you that I would call you."

"But you didn't call and I really want to see you again."

You want to have sex with me again, Christine thought, *but you had your fifteen minutes of fame.*

"I'm sorry," she said. "But we can't see each other any more. I have another boyfriend now."

There was an awkward silence. Finally he mumbled, "Oh. Okay."

"Okay, great," Christine said in a rush. "Now I have to go before Spike gets back. Bye."

Christine hung up the phone. *Another man down.* She and Leonard were similar this way - neither could sustain a relationship for very long. Leonard had made half-assed attempts at relationships with totally inappropriate choices. Sonja was a good example. The women were inevitably dominating and demanding.

Christine, on the other hand, didn't even try to carry any man beyond the fun stage. She enjoyed the dating game and liked the attention of the men who pursued her, but as soon as a relationship moved into a commitment stage, she lost interest. As she watched the marriages of friends go sour and many mean-spirited divorces destroy others' lives, she became more content with her solitary life. The predictable biological urge to have children had not touched her; she had no motherly instincts at all. Contraceptives played an important role in her life.

Christine looked at the phone. *Fuck it; he's not going to phone at this time of night.* She grabbed her parka and drove to the gas station for cigarettes.

———

Leonard had no idea that he was sitting in the crowded emergency waiting room of a Buenos Aires hospital, or that he was sitting next to a Buenos Aires policeman, or that the crying children and moaning people were there for medical treatment. In his foggy and jumbled mind, Leonard was living more than thirty years in the past. He thought he must be in the residential school office, waiting to see Father Ricardo and his infamous leather strap.

He strained to see through his fog. A woman in white appeared. She must be a nun. She signalled an Indian woman to come forward with the boy she was holding on her lap. The boy was bleeding from a large cut on his arm. Two small girls were left behind in their chairs; they were holding hands. Leonard strained his eyes so hard that his head pounded. The girls looked back at him with expressionless faces.

Suddenly everything came into focus. The girls staring at him were Christine and Rosie.

———

Mónica was beginning to get frustrated. "This could be a lot easier for everyone," she said to Andrea, "if you would just co-operate a little. You think Salvador and Ángel are assholes, I think they are assholes."

"I don't know anything," Andrea said in a monotone.

"Well, let me tell you what I know. I know that you allow your home to be used as a safe house for criminals. I know that you know Salvador Juárez and Ángel Méndez. I know that they were at your home minutes before we arrived. And, I know that they would have killed those kids, the Canadian, and probably you, if we hadn't raided it. What I don't know is where they went."

Andrea shrugged her shoulders and kept silent.

"We can protect you."

Andrea shifted uncomfortably in her chair but also remained silent.

"Okay, what about the Canadian?"

"Your people shot him in the head."

"How did he end up with you?"

"I picked him up off the street and brought him home to help him. Is that a crime?"

"No, in fact it's commendable."

"So give me a medal and let me go home."

The door to the interrogation room opened and Horacio stuck his head in. "I think you'd better come out here," he said to Mónica. "We've got a bit of a situation."

As soon as Mónica stepped out in the hallway, she could hear the commotion in the reception area. "What's going on?"

"It's Olivia Cruz's mother - Marcela, - and she has Pedro's uncle, Esteban Lopez, with her."

Mónica's face brightened. "Great. Now we don't have to hunt them down. Bring them into my office."

Mónica had learned a lot about Marcela Cruz in a short time on the police computer files as soon as she had returned to her office after the raid at Andrea's. The woman had lots of reason to rebel - both parents were victims of the Dirty Wars. But Marcela's history showed no signs of rebellion. Raised quietly by her grandfather in the southern Andes, she was a good student. After her young boyfriend had been killed in Las Malvinas, she gave birth to his daughter Olivia. She went to university in Buenos Aires, majoring in fire science, and then working for the Ministry of Environment.

Esteban Lopez, on the other hand, had a very confusing, hard-to-track, seventy-three years. But Mónica had known about Esteban for a long time and had done a lot of tracking. He had first shown up in the system as a guard at Rawson Prison. There was nothing on file, or available, to explain where he had been the forty four years before Rawson. It had been rumoured later, but not verified that he had spent time with Ché Guevara. What interested Mónica was that Esteban had been working at the prison during the mass escape in 1972. An interview transcript, from the day the escape happened, indicated that it was Salvador Juárez who had killed the guard. Why he hadn't shot Salvador Juárez, then and there, was not explained. If he had done so at least three lives would have been saved. Shortly after the nineteen inmates were massacred, Esteban had disappeared off the map again, only to reappear four years later, in 1976, working the family business as if he had never left Buenos Aires thirty years earlier. Mónica knew that Esteban Lopez was still a figure in the underground activist network. But that was insignificant. She didn't care about political manoeuvrings, legal or illegal, she was only interested in his relationship with Salvador Juárez, which she was fairly certain began and ended in 1972.

Her door burst open, and in a second Marcela was on the other side of her desk. "I want my daughter NOW!" she screamed. Esteban and Horacio meekly followed her into the office.

Mónica stood up. "Relax, Miss Cruz, your daughter is fine and she is free to leave."

Horacio pulled two chairs up to the desk. "Please sit down," he said pleasantly.

Marcela settled down immediately with Mónica's assurance, and both she and Esteban sat. "I'm not sure what's going on here," she said, "but I'm certain my daughter has nothing to do with it."

"Yes," Mónica replied, "I'm sure of that also. Horacio, would you please get the kids and bring them here?"

Horacio nodded, "I think they are having a sandwich in the lunch room."

As he left the room, Mónica turned to Esteban. "Mr. Lopez, I'm not so sure that this doesn't involve you."

Esteban put out his arms, "I don't even know what is involved. What happened here? I sent my nephew to deliver empanadas, and he ends up in jail."

"Perhaps you should be more careful where you send him. They were nearly all killed." Mónica became stern. "What do you know about Salvador Juárez?"

Esteban's jaw tightened. "I know that he is murderer and an extortionist, and I would never put anybody I know close to him, especially Pedro or Olivia." His face relaxed and he sat back in his chair. "And besides, I haven't seen Salvador for a long time. We weren't what you would call close friends. My biggest regret in life is that I didn't kill him when I had the chance, in 1972, which was the last time I saw him."

Mónica stared at Esteban hard for a few uncomfortable seconds. "You should regret it," she said finally. "Innocent people lost their lives."

Esteban's face reflected his agreement. "I know," he said. "It haunts me every day."

Mónica turned to Marcela. "What about the Canadian? What's his story?"

"He's a colleague here in Argentina, participating in an international exchange program. He went missing a couple of days ago. I have no idea why he would have been at that house."

"Apparently he was hit by a rubber bullet. Andrea picked him up to help him."

"And," Marcela put out her hands, "Andrea is who?"

"Relevant to this conversation, she is the resident of the house where your colleague was picked up." Mónica turned to Esteban. "And for more information, I'm sure Esteban can fill you in later. We've sent Mr. Frank to the hospital. I think he'll be okay."

The office door opened and Horacio walked in. He was followed by Pedro and Olivia. Marcela immediately jumped to her feet and wrapped her arms around her daughter. Tears streamed down Olivia's face and she kept repeating, "I'm sorry, Mamá. I'm so sorry."

Her mother held her tightly and consoled her. "It's okay, Sweetheart. I'm here now."

Esteban was also up and hugging Pedro. The young man looked truly scared, but he stepped back from Esteban and said, "It was all my fault." He fought back the tears.

Esteban looked at him sympathetically. "No son, it was all my fault."

The phone rang. Mónica picked it up immediately, hoping it would be a hit on Salvador. She had given strict instructions not to be bothered when the door was closed, unless it was urgent. "Yes," she answered. "What is it?"

The dispatcher didn't mince words. "I've just got a call from the hospital. The Canadian just kidnapped two young girls and is on the run."

———

Leonard's stunned and fuzzy mind had awakened and now was operating clearly and distinctly as Lenny, twelve year-old on the run. He held Christine with one arm and dragged Rosie by the hand with the other. Both girls were crying hysterically as he ran down the city sidewalk, dodging and sometimes running into startled pedestrians.

He could see trees and a field ahead, like the view from his dormitory window. He headed directly towards it.

"It's okay," he assured his sisters with heavy breaths. "It's okay now." He could feel his heart pounding and his injured forehead throbbing. He needed to rest, but first he needed to get Christine and Rosie to a safe place. This would be his only opportunity and he could not fail.

He stopped at the edge of the field. The sisters' faces were wet from tears and they were too traumatized to struggle against his dragging them along. Still, he was breathing heavily and dripping with sweat. He looked to a line of trees along a creek ravine approximately a hundred metres across the open field. He needed to get the girls there. They needed cover.

Between them and the trees were park benches and sidewalks. It was early in the morning so there were not many people - one couple on a bench and some kids kicking a ball. Leonard pulled the girls the long way around the field to avoid the couple's attention. They had to pass closer to the soccer game, but the attention there was on the ball. He dragged the crying sisters directly to the tree line, where a bridge crossed the creek ravine. He slid down the bank, clutching Christine and pulling Rosie down under the bridge where he was sure they couldn't be seen. He sat down and squeezed them tight against his chest.

His vision was clearer now and he could see that his sisters were terrified. "It's okay now," he tried to console them. "I won't let them take you again."

——

Salvador ordered Ángel to park the small stolen Renault inconspicuously, so they could see the police station but would not be noticed as they waited. Salvador had shaved his beard, cut his hair and donned sunglasses. Ángel had pulled a knitted hat down over his ears, hiding his shaved head, and wore sunglasses.

"I don't like this at all," Ángel said nervously.

Salvador kept his eyes trained on the police station door. "Don't worry," he said. "This is the last place they would look for us, or for a stolen car. I want to see who comes out of there. This could be a good opportunity."

"Or an incredibly big mistake." Ángel's fingers were drumming on the steering wheel. "We could be a long way from here."

"This whole thing was set up by Esteban Lopez, using that bitch at the house and his nephew." Salvador rubbed at the scar on his temple. "He tried to stop me at Rawson, and he's trying to stop me now."

"That was thirty years ago," Ángel complained.

Salvador didn't reply. He slipped out a pistol from under his seat and checked the bullet chamber.

——

Mónica stood with Marcela and her entourage at the reception counter. Only Ernesto stood off to the side, seemingly unaffected and chatting with a policewoman. "Okay," Mónica said, "I've got an all-points bulletin out and we have every policeman in the city looking. This shouldn't take long. You can all go home and relax. As soon as we find them, we'll let you know."

"It was your trigger-happy policemen that put him in this situation," Marcela said. "They better not hurt him again."

"He has two girls with him. I've ordered that no shots are to be fired."

Olivia jumped into the conversation. "He didn't even know who I was, Mother. I don't think he even knows where he's at, or who he is."

Marcela agreed. "Leonard would not hurt the girls. He must be delusional and somehow thinking he's helping them."

Mónica returned her attention to the more pressing concern. "Esteban, if you're serious about hating Salvador, I would like you and Andrea to stay and talk for a while. I think that maybe you could be an asset to my investigation."

Esteban shrugged his shoulders. "I don't have a problem with that, but I don't see how we can help."

Mónica was not sure that they could help either, but she was not going to leave any stone unturned. And she was intrigued with Esteban

Lopez. She knew who he was on paper, and she had loathed him for being such a coward in 1972 and not killing Salvador when he had a legal opportunity. But now that she had met Esteban, she found him likable and compassionate. She put a friendly hand on his shoulder. "Let's get to work and see."

———

Salvador instinctively tightened his grip on the loaded pistol when he saw that Esteban's nephew and his girlfriend were part of the group leaving the police station. The four of them walked directly towards him and Ángel. He slowly pulled back the trigger to the cocked position. He could feel his adrenalin start to flow. His mouth was dry and the palms of his hands wet. The group kept up their pace towards him, and he calculated which ones he would take out first. He had six shots and four targets. It would be close range, but the first shot would throw everything into chaos. He decided it would be Pedro. That way, if he couldn't get another, at least he would have caused the most collateral damage. By shooting the boy, he would be shooting Esteban through the heart.

Salvador's target was no more than five metres from his window when he felt Ángel's hand on his arm. He turned and glared. Ángel kept the pressure on his arm. The group walked past their car, only six inches from Salvador, and got into the car parked immediately behind them.

"Not here," Ángel finally spoke. "It would be suicide. I have no escape route and no plan."

Behind smouldering eyes, Salvador was already making a plan. "Follow them," he ordered. "This could be our day."

———

Marcela had no intention of going home to relax, as the detective had suggested. Not when Leonard was living a nightmare. "We're going to the hospital," she said matter-of-factly.

"I knew that," Ernesto answered.

"What are we going to do?" Olivia asked. "He could be any place in the city."

"I want to know exactly what happened there," Marcela said. "Talk to anybody who might have seen what happened. I doubt that in his condition, and moving with two little girls, he would get very far. Maybe we can get to him before the police do."

"That would be good," Olivia said. "Maybe we can save him!"

Marcela could hear the growing excitement in her daughter's voice. "We still have to talk," she cautioned. "But that's later. How are you two doing now?"

"We're fine," Olivia answered for both. "Although I don't think I ever want to spend another minute in a jail."

"How you got there in the first place is something we'll talk about later."

Pedro spoke up for the first time. "It was my fault, Miss Cruz."

Ernesto's salsa-themed ring tone ended the conversation. "*Hola*," he answered. "Ernesto de Salvo, *hombre* extraordinaire." He listened with a question marking his expression, then spoke in English: "He's not available right now. Can I take a message? … Marcela? … Yes, she's available. Can I tell her who's speaking? … Okay, just a moment." He put his hand over the mouth-piece as he handed it to Marcela. "It's Leonard's sister - Christine."

"Shit," Marcela whispered, and took the phone. "Hello, this is Marcela Cruz."

"Hello, Marcela. My name is Christine Frank. My brother is Leonard Frank."

"He's told me much about you, Christine."

"Well, don't believe any of it. I'm actually beautiful and smart." There was a pause. "Marcela, Leonard was supposed to phone me last night and I still haven't heard from him. Do you know how I can get in touch with him? I hate to be a pain in the ass, but—"

"No," Marcela cut her off. "No, it's fine. Actually, Christine, we do have a bit of a problem. Seems that Leonard was hit in the head with a rubber bullet during a demonstration and was taken to some kind of dissident safe house. This house ended up getting raided by the police, who put Leonard, my daughter and a couple of others in jail. They did take Leonard to the hospital, but it seems he's kidnapped a couple of little girls and we're looking for him now."

As soon as she had finished speaking, there was silence on the line. Marcela realized what she had just said. "That didn't sound very good, did it, Christine?"

"Are we talking about Leonard Frank, from Canada?"

"I'm sorry, Christine," Marcela tried to mend the damage. "I didn't intend to be so blunt. I'm sure that all this will be cleared up very soon, probably in the next couple of hours. Give me your phone number, and I'll call you back as soon as I know more."

"Should I be getting on a plane, Marcela?"

"No, don't worry. I'll definitely phone you tonight."

Christine gave Marcela her number, and they agreed to talk again at six o'clock.

———

Mónica wanted to hear whatever Esteban could tell her. He would be able to fill in some holes in Salvador's history and the history of the events of 1972. She decided to have Andrea involved in the discussion. Andrea had been with Salvador just hours ago; maybe together they would feel more comfortable. Mónica knew that intimidation would not work. Neither of these two would react well to threats, and this wasn't the time to use the good cop/bad cop technique. Only a good cop would be able to get co-operation from Esteban. If he felt comfortable, then Andrea too would relax her guard. Mónica was only trying to extract helpful information from them, not a confession.

She decided the interview would take place in the lunch room, over *maté* and *tortas fritas* to make things more casual. She gave orders to the policewoman at the reception desk that they were not to be interrupted.

Once they were all seated around the table and Horacio took on the duty of pouring the hot water, Mónica began in a friendly tone of voice. "I want to thank both of you for taking the time to talk with me. I want to be clear that my intention here is only to get a better idea of what I can expect from Salvador as a criminal and perhaps stop him from killing or kidnapping another innocent person. I don't have any political agenda, and I could care less about your political position. Also, I have no interest in any laws that either of you may have compromised now, or in the past. My only interest is in putting Salvador away for good."

Esteban sat back in his chair and crossed his arms. "This sounds like it might be a little personal for you."

Mónica took a sip of *maté*. "It is," she confessed. "I have been on his case for my entire career and getting nowhere. So yes, I want Juárez." She passed the *maté* back to Horacio. He refilled the cup with hot water and passed it on to Andrea.

"I don't have any reason to protect him," Esteban said. "I don't like him, and we really don't have any affiliation with him."

Mónica looked directly at Esteban. "Why didn't you shoot him at Rawson when you had the chance?"

Esteban leaned back, stunned, as if hit on the forehead. "I should have killed him," he said finally, shifting uncomfortably in his chair. "I hit him over the head and knocked him out. His head was split open bad and I thought he was dead. There was a lot of confusion and everything happened fast. He killed my sister's boyfriend - and who knows how many more." He shook his head in grief. "I should have done more."

Mónica didn't console him. "Yes, you should have done more." She turned her attention to Andrea. "How did he end up at your house?"

"He was referred there by a friend." She tossed Esteban a nervous glance.

"Don't worry, Andrea," Mónica said quickly. "Remember, the only thing I'm interested in is getting Salvador. Nothing else. I need to know everything now. The more time he has, the less chance we have of taking him off the street."

Andrea's tense features seem to relax, and Esteban gave her a nod. "He and Ángel showed up in the middle of the night," she began. "They gave me the name Vicky Moreno, a lady who stayed with me before, and I let them in. They told me in no uncertain terms that nobody was to know they were there." She turned to Esteban. "I wanted to tell you, but—"

Esteban waved her. "Don't worry about it."

She continued. "The next day they made plans to get involved with the demonstrations and I offered to help. Once we were actually out on the street, I could see that they only wanted to incite violence. When the police showed up with guns and batons, we ran. The Canadian got hit in the crossfire. I recognized him as a friend of Esteban's, so I insisted we help him."

"Do you know who warned Salvador that we were coming to your house?"

Andrea shook her head. "No, I don't have any idea, but the barrio has a thousand eyes. Salvador got a call on his cell phone and him and Ángel were out the back door."

Mónica turned to Esteban. "Is there anything you can add? Where do you think he would run?"

Esteban shrugged his shoulders. "I don't really know him, but I would guess that he doesn't run scared and makes his escape plan spontaneously, so he's pretty much the only one who has any idea of where he's going. I doubt he'll leave the city, though."

"What do you think his primary motivation is?" Mónica asked. "From my research, I would guess that in the end it is money. He wants to help promote political chaos and then capitalize on it."

"That would certainly be high on the list," Esteban agreed. "And from his history, I would think that he craves famous notoriety. But personally I think revenge takes even a higher spot. I was told, by people who would know, that when the foreign minister was killed in 1974, it was only because he had said something bad about Salvador in a television interview. Not for the political reasons that were published."

"He thinks you set up the raid," Andrea said to Esteban.

"I would have, if I'd known he was there."

"How do you know that?" Mónica asked Andrea, sensing that this might be helpful.

Andrea didn't see any significance. "Because when Pedro showed up and I told Salvador that this was Esteban's nephew, he instantly turned angry and was ready to kill Pedro just for being related to Esteban. When he was warned about the raid on my house, he immediately figured that Pedro and Olivia were part of a set-up."

The realization swept over the room like a cold wind: Salvador would go after Pedro and Olivia. Horacio jumped to his feet, Mónica took the phone in her hand and Esteban could only utter: "Son of a bitch!"

——

Marcela walked into the chaos of the emergency waiting area. Olivia, Pedro and Ernesto followed closely behind. The room was already at capacity, filled with moaning patients, scurrying nurses, idle policemen and a policewoman consoling a near-hysterical mother. The air was thick with the pungent smell of sickness, medicines and fear.

"My God." Marcela put her hand to her mouth. "What a mess."

"I'll wander around and ask some questions," Ernesto said.

"I'd better talk to the police and the little girls' mother," Marcela sighed.

"This place is going to make me sick." Olivia said, making a sour face. "Pedro and I will be outside. We'll ask if anyone saw where they went."

"Don't go far. We may need to leave soon."

——

Salvador couldn't believe his luck. "So, my Christmas present comes a few days early," he sneered as he watched Pedro and the girl leave the hospital alone. "It's even gift wrapped and delivered."

"Do you have some sort of plan?" Ángel asked. "Because if I am a part of it, then I want to know that a workable escape is also part of it. Let's try to avoid prison."

"I will *never* go back to prison," Salvador spat out.

"Well, let's not get killed, either. This isn't worth it."

"Just keep close to them. When they are at a good spot, we'll take them."

"What'd you mean, *take them?*" Ángel demanded. "Are you talking kidnap them or kill them?"

Salvador grinned. "Probably both."

—

Leonard had an arm around each girl and squeezed them in tightly. It was dark and damp under the bridge, and they were cramped on a steep dirt bank. Christine wouldn't stop crying. Two teenage boys were passing along the creek under the bridge, kicking a soccer ball and laughing. When they saw Leonard crouched down with the girls, they hesitated and then continued as if they didn't notice.

"Christine, please try to be quiet," he pleaded. "We don't want the priest to find us."

Rosie was sobbing softly. "*Hable español*," she said through her tears.

"Don't worry, Rosie," he whispered. "I'll get us home."

—

August 1, 1966
Northern British Columbia, Canada

Lenny was becoming concerned about his little sister. They had been moving north for two weeks and Christine was exhausted. They had followed the road but stayed concealed in the bush as much as they could. They had no money, and there were no phones at Long Lake Indian Reserve to call for help. They lived off grouse, berries and whatever Lenny could steal from gardens and other people's garbage. He was resigned to the fact that they would have to walk the entire distance home. The only point of reference he had was that the residential school was one long day in a car driving south from the reserve. So, they walked north, following

Highway 16 towards the city of Prince George, where Lenny remembered they had stopped on the way to the school and had seen lots of Indians on the sidewalks. Maybe two Indian children alone on the street would go unnoticed here, he thought as they limped down the main street. And maybe the other Indians will give us some money.

The first Indian he saw was a girl on the corner in a very short dress and with not very much covering her breasts. She also had a lot of face paint on her lips and around her eyes.

"She looks nice," Lenny whispered to Christine. "Let's ask her for help."

He took Christine's hand and approached the girl. She was smoking a cigarette and looked down at them as they stopped in front of her. She exhaled smoke in Lenny's face, and before he could say a word she said, "Fuck off, kid."

Lenny led Christine away in a hurry. He was out of his element here. He had no idea of who was good and who was bad. They walked quickly down the street, past the hotels and bars. Lenny noticed that there were several girls on the sidewalk who looked similar to the mean girl who'd blown smoke on them. He also noticed that most of the Indian men he saw appeared to be very drunk - something that he sometimes saw on the reserve, but never in the house. His parents didn't drink.

Eventually he and Christine got to a part of town where there were more stores than bars or hotels, and they saw fewer painted ladies and stumbling drunks. Seeing a sign that said "Northern Hardware," Lenny remembered his father mentioning the store as an unbelievable place that had anything anybody could want. Lenny had no money, but he felt drawn to the store, if only to look at everything.

He led Christine, who was uncharacteristically silent, inside the store. They walked up and down the aisles, looking at all the items, but careful not to touch anything. There were Chestnut snowshoes, leg-hold traps, wringer washing machines and, like his father had said, everything Lenny could imagine. And it was all shiny and new. Neither Lenny, nor Christine had ever seen anything like it.

After they had walked, wide-eyed, up and down every aisle of the store three times, Lenny tugged on his little sister's arm as she gawked wistfully at the fishing supplies. "Let's go, Christine. We need to find a place to stay tonight."

Christine frowned. "I don't want to leave," she said weakly. "I want to stay here forever."

Lenny put his hand on her shoulder, feeling compassion for his little sister. She was nearly broken. This wasn't what she deserved from life. She was like a snowshoe rabbit, one who could never be an Easter bunny. She needed to be all over the place at once, with her ears up and sniffing the air. He had to get her home before it was too late.

"I promise I'll bring you here again someday, and you'll be able to get anything you want."

Christine smiled weakly. "I'd get Mommy that gasoline-powered wringer washer."

"Hey, that's not the sister that I know!" Lenny cracked, trying to bring some life to her. "You aren't thinking of yourself."

"I know," Christine admitted. "But I'm tired, and it takes too much energy to think of myself."

Lenny laughed. "That's because you're hard to please."

"Let's go," Christine sighed, "before it gets dark."

"Leonard?" A man's strong voice spoke out. "Christine?"

Lenny grabbed his sister's hand and tensed his muscles to run out of the store.

The voice came from behind them.

"Leonard!" This time it wasn't a question, but a demand.

Lenny turned to the voice just as he was ready to spring. The only thought going through his head was that they must not be caught and sent back to the school. He would do anything to stop that.

It took a few seconds to register in his tired brain.

An Indian with a white woman.

Uncle John!

Lenny's knees went weak. It was over. They were safe! Uncle John, their father's youngest brother, was the smartest guy in the family. He could read and write and speak English well, and he had a job at the asbestos mine in Cassiar, near the Yukon border. He was married to a French lady, Aunt Josette, from Quebec. Before Lenny could catch his breath, his uncle and aunt were kneeling next to them, then holding them and hugging them. They were in safe hands now.

"We've been looking everywhere for you!" Uncle John was nearly crying. "Where have you been for the last two weeks?"

Lenny and Christine were both too stunned to reply.

Josette hugged Christine tightly against her chest. "We can talk later," she said. "Let's get these kids to the motel."

Christine spoke up, "I want to see Mommy and Daddy."

Time seemed to suddenly stop.

Lenny could feel it.

Uncle John looked as if he'd been kicked in the chest, and Josette's face dropped.

"What?" Lenny asked, repressing the panic he was feeling. "What's wrong?"

Josette stood and picked up Christine. "Let's just get to the motel, and you can take a nice bath."

Lenny kept his eyes on his uncle. He needed to know.

Uncle John just stood there; avoiding Lenny's stare, and put out his hand.

Lenny took his uncle's hand. They followed Josette and Christine out onto the main street of Prince George and into a new phase of their lives.

CHAPTER NINE

Mónica had whipped the police station into a frenzy. Several officers were busy donning bullet-proof vests, adjusting helmets and checking over their weapons. Mónica selected a Ruger Redhawk .357 magnum from the gun locker and slipped it into her bag. When she looked up she saw that Horacio was watching her with a frown that said, *Isn't that too big of a gun?* She responded with a quick shrug and put on her own vest.

Horacio turned and spoke out loud to the officers. "Okay men, we have two objectives. The most important one is to secure the safety of Olivia Cruz and Pedro Lopez. The second objective is to find and apprehend Salvador Juárez and Ángel Méndez. Any questions?

"Yes sir," one officer spoke up. "Can we shoot to kill?"

"If it's absolutely necessary," Horacio said.

Mónica went to the dispatcher's window. "I want units at Esteban's and Marcela's. And I want the all-points bulletin extended in those neighbourhoods. Did you try to call Marcela's home yet?"

"Yes sir, ah, I mean, yes ma'am," the young dispatcher stammered. "No answer."

"Keep trying. What about Esteban's?"

"Two units are already there, but no sign of Pedro."

"Tell them to find a good location and watch the place. Salvador could show up there."

A policewoman approached Mónica with a business card in her hand. "The driver gave me his cell number," she said with a tinge of embarrassment.

Mónica snatched the card from her hand and gave it directly to the dispatcher. "Get him on the line and put it through to my office phone."

——

Olivia held onto Pedro's arm as they walked away from the hospital. It was the first time they had been alone since it all began behind Andrea's house.

"You're shaking," Pedro told her.

"Everything seems to be catching up with me," Olivia replied, her voice cracking. "We were nearly killed."

"But we survived, Amor." Pedro put his arm around her shoulder and squeezed her in tight. "Now we just have to survive your mother's wrath."

"She's also scared."

"Maybe we can find the Canadian and be heroes."

"I just want to go home." Olivia's voice was weak.

Pedro pointed to a magazine and flower vendor on the corner, "I know the guy at the kiosk over there. His name is Gustavo. He's another person that I bring empanadas to. Esteban gets flowers in return, and we put them on the tables when we have a special night."

"I've always wondered where they came from," Olivia said.

"Let's talk to him. Maybe he saw something."

——

Salvador had never in his life felt a stronger sense that the universe was unfolding as it should than he had at this moment watching Pedro and Olivia walk hand in hand. "There's a park a couple of blocks in the direction they're heading," he told Ángel. "If they get that far, we'll have them and nobody will know."

Ángel shook his head. "We could be half-way to Patagonia right now and for sure nobody would know."

"I can't believe that you're too stupid to see the opportunity we have here. In one shot, we get hostages, then we get money, then we get Esteban."

"I don't give a shit about Esteban. That's your ghost."

"You can do your job and be in for half the take, or you can get out of the car now and be a coward with no money and no future."

Ángel was silent, except for his fingers drumming the steering wheel. He watched Pedro and the girl. They had stopped at a corner magazine stand. The vendor greeted them and they talked for a couple of minutes. Then the vendor pointed in the direction they had been walking, and the happy couple moved on.

"Follow them." Salvador was firm.

Ángel made his decision. He put the car into gear and took his foot off the brake.

———

Marcela had reassured the distressed mother of the kidnapped girls that they would not be hurt. She had consoled the mother's son with the bandaged arm and she had talked to the investigating police officer. All she found out was that the policeman watching Leonard had nodded off in the heat and stench of the emergency waiting room - for no more than a couple of minutes, he insisted. When he opened his eyes, Leonard and the two little girls were gone. The others were too focused on their own pain to notice, and the little girls protests were most likely drowned out with the cries of the injured. Nobody saw, or heard, anything. Maybe Olivia had discovered something outside the hospital.

Marcela went to Ernesto, who had spent the entire time talking with a pretty doll-like nurse. She cut directly into their conversation: "Have you found out anything *useful*?"

Ernesto's smile evaporated. He gave Marcela a puzzled look, and then his salsa ring tone sounded, as if on cue. "Ernesto de Salvo," he answered and then he handed the phone to Marcela. "It's the detective."

"Yes, this is Marcela." She listened for a moment. Her eyes opened wide, she dropped the phone and ran for the door.

———

Olivia and Pedro headed toward the park where Gustavo, the street vender, had seen Leonard bring the two little girls. He had said they attracted his attention because the girls seemed to be putting up so much resistance. A child being a pain in the ass for their parents was not an unusual occurrence on the city streets, but both kids putting up such a fight was enough for the vendor to look up from his newspaper for a moment.

This information excited Olivia. It took her mind and emotions from the horror of the last sixteen hours and gave her some optimism. "If we can find Leonard and the children playing in the park, it would sure put a happy ending to this situation," she said.

"Let's hurry," Pedro said, and picked up the pace. "Maybe they haven't gotten far."

They walked quickly to the park and a point where they had a broad view of the walkways, lawns and field. They stopped and gazed over the area. The manicured grass was divided with sidewalks of inlaid stone, carved wooden benches and small brick lined flower beds. A couple of boys kicked a soccer ball back and forth near a statue of Eva Peron.

"I don't see anything," Pedro said.

"Let's go talk to those boys," Olivia suggested. "They might have seen something."

As they approached the teenagers, the ball escaped the boys and bounced towards Pedro. He deftly kicked the ball straight up, bounced it on his head and then kicked it back to the red-haired boy. The boy thanked him and continued playing with his friend.

"Excuse me," Olivia said. "Can you help us for a second?"

The boys stopped the ball immediately and the red-haired kid replied, "What do you want?"

"We are looking for a friend of ours who has two little girls with him. We're pretty sure that they came through here. Have you seen anybody like that?"

The boys looked at each other and then red-hair pointed to a bridge crossing on the far edge of the park. "We saw a man with two girls under that bridge. The little girls were crying."

Olivia thanked them and headed directly for the bridge.

———

Leonard pleaded with the girls to stop crying. "Please Rosie, they are going to find us and take us back."

The girl looked back at Leonard. She was nearly hysterical. Her hair was tangled and her face dripping with tears. Suddenly, she yelled directly at Leonard, *"Habla español!"* and without warning slapped his face. *"No entiendo!"*

The girl's reaction caught Leonard completely off guard. His cheek stung and his vision blurred. He was about to recover when she slapped him soundly a second time. *"Habla español!"* she screamed into his face.

He opened his eyes. Rosie's face looked different. It was the face of a girl he had never seen before. He turned to Christine, but it wasn't his little sister. He put his head in his hands, trying to think clearly.

———

Salvador saw that his opportunity had arrived, as if he had meticulously planned every facet, scheduled every step. In fact, he knew that he couldn't have planned things any better than they were going. Every plan has points where things can go in unplanned directions, where alternatives have to be considered and implemented on the spot, usually resulting in chaos and failure. This was not one of those times.

Salvador didn't even have to think; he just had to accept his role in the events that were unfolding.

"Okay," he whispered to Ángel. "This is it. I'll come up behind them as they reach that creek near the tree line, and hold them with the gun. I expect you to be there with the car immediately. Do you understand?"

Ángel nodded. He was committed now. He saw that they would be able to slip away without being seen, and maybe would even be able to extort some cash in the end. "I'll be there," he assured Salvador. "Don't worry about me."

Salvador checked the gun cylinder one more time and tucked it in his pants. He was ready. It was time to stop thinking and start acting. He got out of the car and, with his right hand gripping the pistol, took up a fast pace behind Pedro and the girl. Glancing around, he saw there were no witnesses.

As they neared the creek and the tree line, Salvador picked up his pace so that he was nearly running. A loud screech of rubber tires sounded suddenly behind him violating the serenity of the park and interrupting the flow of his plan.

He whirled around to see police cars arriving from every direction. Ángel was getting out of the car, with his hands held high. Several heavily armed and armoured police ran to him and threw Ángel face down on the ground. More police cars with sirens arrived.

A man and a woman with bullet-proof vests over street clothes sprang from the lead car and, with guns drawn, began running towards Salvador. He turned and found himself facing Pedro and the girl, who had also turned their attention to the commotion. Instinctively and without thought, he stepped behind the girl, grabbed a handful of her hair and put the gun to her head.

He yelled at Pedro, "Down on the ground or I'll fucking blow her apart!" Pedro was immediately on the ground with his hands out. The armed man and woman had stopped their approach, but still had their weapons trained on Salvador. "I'll fucking kill her!" he screamed at them.

"It's all over, Salvador!" the woman yelled. "Drop the gun!"

"If you know my name," he yelled back, "then you know that I will kill her without a thought."

"Oh, I know your name," the woman said, "and maybe you should know my name."

"Your name doesn't make any difference to me," Salvador laughed out. "We aren't going to be friends."

"My name is Detective Mónica Garcia," she told him. "And I am not your friend." Her gun remained pointed at his head.

"Pleased to meet you, Detective." He pulled the girl's hair back for effect. "But right now, I don't really give a shit."

"Daughter of Eduardo Garcia!" Mónica yelled with strength and passion, so that there was no question.

Salvador felt a blow to his solar plexus, as though he had been kicked in the chest. The friendly face of the Rawson taxi driver flashed through his consciousness; the face of the second and last man Salvador had actually killed. Since then, he had delegated any killing that had to be done to the young guys who were out to make a mark. Salvador was only out to make money. He had shot the guard thirty years ago because it needed to be done to assist the escape. He had killed the taxi driver in a rush of adrenalin and out of vicious bravado. Once he had calmed down and realized the stupidity of his act, he found that the image of Eduardo Garcia's gracious face, and Garcia's plea, were embedded in his consciousness: *I have a ten-year-old daughter who has no mother!*

A woman suddenly broke out from the police line and ran towards Salvador. "Let her go!" the woman screamed. "That's my daughter!"

The man with Mónica lowered his gun and caught the charging woman. He held her back while she continued to scream and fight his grip.

"I will kill her!" Salvador yelled at the crazed mother. "Ask Señora Garcia. I killed her father!"

Salvador caught a movement from Pedro, who was taking a step towards Salvador. Without hesitating he levelled the gun barrel at the boy's chest and pulled the trigger. The boy spun around from the force of the bullet and landed face-down in the dirt. The girl screamed like a dying animal and jolted to her boyfriend, leaving Salvador holding a handful of hair. He pointed the gun at the girl to shoot, when a thundering blow shattered his eardrum and crushed his cheek bones. He dropped to his knees and looked in the direction the blow had come from. With blurring vision, he could make out the injured man from Andrea's safe house, standing over him with a heavy wooden pole.

That son of a bitch! Where did he come from?

He lifted his pistol weakly towards the man.

Then Salvador saw the lower part of his arm fall down helplessly. Simultaneously he felt the .357 magnum bullet disintegrating his elbow. Things were not making sense.

The last thing he saw, before consciousness slipped away, was the face of Eduardo Garcia's daughter, twisted with hate, behind the hot gun barrel that was burning a zero into his forehead.

December 10, 1982
Buenos Aires Police Academy, Argentina

Mónica Garcia sat in the first row, front and centre with the top ten percent of the Class of 82 Police Academy graduation ceremony. None of her family was there to see her accomplishment, but it didn't take any pride away from the moment. She would have loved for her father to be present - but then, if he had been alive, she probably wouldn't be sitting there. She wouldn't have had the all-encompassing drive to bring murderers to justice. Perhaps she would have been a doctor, chasing after a cure for the lung cancer that took her mother, or a scientist, or maybe even a housewife with a bunch of kids. It didn't matter. She was happy and proud to be sitting where she was, even if there was only one other person that cared.

That one other person was Father Enrique, from the orphanage where Mónica had spent eight years. He became her guiding light only days after her father had been murdered. She was only ten years old when it had happened, and until then her father had been her hero and the one who had held her together after her mother died. Mónica had been a devastated little girl when she was turned over to the orphanage and Father Enrique had taken her under his wing. He turned her devastation into determination. He was the one who had planted the seed for her career in the administration of justice, and who then had tended her education until she bloomed into the proud flower in the front row.

She had found Father Enrique in the audience. He was beaming as if she were his own daughter. She smiled for him because she knew how much he loved her smile, and also because it was the happiest time of her life. He told her that her mother and father were there with her also, and she could feel their presence. Everything that had happened in her life, all her pain and suffering, all her ability to focus intently on a goal, and most of Father Enrique's time and money, were coming together today. She savoured every sound, every sight and smell. She felt and acknowledged every emotion that washed over her.

This was her day!

Tomorrow it would be time to put her skills and focus to work.

Tomorrow she would help to bring justice to the world.

———

Mónica wanted to pull the trigger almost more than she cared to have a life. The man who had destroyed her family and put her in an orphanage was lying on his back, unconscious, his arm blown apart by her bullet and his face made unrecognizable by Leonard's big stick. With a simple squeeze of a finger, it would all be over. Her life would be complete. Mission accomplished.

She felt a hand on her shoulder and looked up to see Horacio towering over her. He nodded in the direction of the street. The television cameras and the news people were already flooding the scene and getting footage. "It's all over, Mónica." He spoke with the gentle voice of a friend. "It's over," he repeated and held his hand out to her. She could taste the salt of her tears as they touched her parched lips. She could feel the blood running through her veins and the energy encompassing her soul. She accepted Horacio's hand and stood.

Looking around, she saw a scene of head-spinning activity. Paramedics with stretchers were rushing onto the scene to attend to Pedro, who was alive but bleeding badly, and Leonard, who had dropped to his knees after clubbing Salvador. Marcela was frantic over Olivia, who was more than frantic over Pedro. The police swarmed over the area like black locusts, trying to control the invading journalists.

A movement beyond the scene caught Mónica's eye. Two little girls, holding hands, dishevelled and tear-stained, appeared from under the bridge.

CHAPTER TEN

Day Five
December 22, 2001

Leonard sat on Marcela's couch resting with his eyes closed and his consciousness safely back in present-day Buenos Aires. His head injury had been tended to at the hospital, and Marcela would not entertain any talk of him returning to his motel room. She had already picked up his belongings from the motel and put them in her room. She said that she would sleep with Olivia.

He had bathed in Marcela's bathtub until the water became lukewarm, and then changed into fresh clothes. The scents of freshly picked lavender and burning candles pleasantly flavoured the air of her tiny apartment. She had put on some soft music discreetly in the background.

Marcela came from the bedroom wearing a light cotton dress and sat beside him.

"How are you doing?" she asked.

Leonard opened his eyes and smiled. "I'm doing good," he replied. "Thank you for everything."

Marcela smiled and Leonard saw her as the most beautiful woman that ever existed. "Did I tell you that I talked to your sister?"

Leonard's smile flattened out. "Christine? No, you didn't. Did you happen to mention anything?" he asked reluctantly.

Marcela looked embarrassed. "I think I might have mentioned everything."

"Everything?"

Marcela nodded, "Everything."

"Even - "

"Everything."

"Okay," Leonard said. "She's going to be a little freaked out for awhile."

"I'm sorry, Leonard. I thought, she's you're sister, she needs to know."

"No, it's good that you told her. But I can imagine how she reacted."

Marcela laughed. "She was going to get on a plane."

Leonard laid his head back and closed his eyes. He imagined Christine going crazy because she didn't know exactly what had happened. He would have to call her today. If he didn't call, she would be on the next plane to Argentina for sure.

———

Olivia sat on Pedro's hospital bed and stroked his hand. He was her man, her hero. And there was no way she would leave his side. She hadn't been able to stay the night, as he was in surgery. The bullet had hit him just below the collar bone and came out through his back without causing any major damage. But Olivia was at the hospital at six in the morning and had made such a ruckus that the nursing staff allowed her in.

Pedro's eyes slightly opened for the first time.

"*Pobrecito*," she whispered, "*mi amor, mi vida.*"

Pedro smiled weakly. "I'm still alive?"

"Yes, *mi amor*, you are still alive."

"What happened?"

"If it wasn't for you trying to protect me, I would have surely gotten killed."

"All I remember is Salvador saying he would kill you and I made one step towards you."

"When you lunged for his gun, he got a lucky shot off and caught you in the shoulder. You were going to come back at him, when Mr. Frank came from behind and hit Salvador with a big stick. That knocked him to his knees but not out. Detective Garcia shot him and blew his arm off."

"Did you get hurt?" Pedro asked.

"No, *mi vida*." Olivia smiled. "You saved me. You're my hero."

"Maybe your mother will go easier on me now," Pedro joked.

"I hope that she'll go easier on both of us. But I wouldn't count on it."

———

Marcela passed the *maté* to Leonard. "Most gringos put *yerba maté* in the same classification as cow shit," she warned him.

Leonard took the small gourd and straightened out the silver straw, the *bombilla*. "You make it sound so good." He was looking examining the contents, which definitely had the appearance and consistency of fresh cow shit. He took a small sip. Marcela had added a bit of sugar to make the initial sips more palatable for the first-time user.

"That's not so bad. I could get used to it." He took another sip and handed it back to her. "The sugar makes it taste like sweet cow shit," he said and grinned.

Marcela poured more hot water into the *maté* and sipped from the *bombilla*. She liked it when Leonard smiled. It wasn't just a facial expression with him, it was happiness.

After a few seconds of silence, his expression turned serious and Marcela could see his jaw tense. "I'm sorry to have put you and Olivia through all this," he said finally. "With all the things going on here right now, you didn't need this."

She waved him off. "Don't worry about it. It was fate, which neither you nor I have any control over."

"I wish that I could look at it as a matter of fate."

"You will, eventually," she assured him.

The phone rang, and Marcela got up to answer it. "It's probably Olivia," she guessed. "I asked her to call to let us know how Pedro is doing."

"Hola," she answered in a sing-song voice.

"Can you tell me just what the hell is going on?"

Marcela's happy face tightened into a defensive position. It was Diego, and he wasn't using his happy voice. She had forgotten all about her boss; in fact, she hadn't given a single thought to her job for the last two insane days.

"What do you mean?" Marcela asked innocently.

"You know fucking well what I mean!" Diego thundered back. "The television and the newspapers have blasted it over the entire fucking country! Our Canadian is a hero, single-handedly catching the number one criminal in Argentina! And I don't know a single fucking thing about it! How do you think that makes me look?"

Marcela didn't have any excuses prepared. "I'm sorry that I didn't call you," she said calmly, "but it just happened and we're still catching our breath."

"Where is he now?"

"Sitting here next to me."

"Let me talk to him."

Marcela handed the phone to Leonard and silently mouthed, "Diego."

Leonard silently mouthed "Shit" and took the phone. "Hello …I'm fine, si..." Leonard was using a casual, no-problems-here voice. "No problem, sir. We'll have Ernesto get us there by two o'clock … Okay, I'll talk to you then, sir … Okay, here she is, sir, I mean Diego." Leonard passed the phone back to Marcela with a shrug.

"Yes?" Marcela knew that Diego had something over her now, and that he would exploit it.

"Make sure both of you are here at two o'clock," he ordered sharply.

"No problem," Marcela answered in English. She hung up the phone and turned on the little television on the counter. "I guess we should watch the news," she suggested. "It's all in Spanish, but I'm sure you'll get the idea."

The little television popped on with a video shot of Plaza de Mayo. Children in shorts were playing in the fountain pool, and old men were feeding corn to the pigeons. There were a few hundred people milling about, and small groups of protesters gathered here and there, with the majestic pink presidential palace in the background. At the top of the palace, a huge Argentine flag, whipped by a constant Atlantic breeze, exhibited a happy yellow sun shining between light blue stripes. Below the rippling flag, black-clad police were lined up in front of the presidential palace and scattered in a loose grid covering the plaza. The scene appeared to be a *very* secure day in the park. An off-camera reporter described the scene.

There was relative calm in Buenos Aires and elsewhere yesterday, in contrast to the riots and looting of the past four days. But it has been a tense waiting period as power passed from the Radical party president, Fernando de la Rua, to the opposition Peronists after three days of social unrest, widespread looting and police repression that has left 27 people dead and more than 150 wounded.

The scene changed abruptly to the same shot of the Plaza de Mayo, but now packed with tens of thousands of chanting, yelling, pot-banging protesters. There were no children playing in the fountain and no free space on the ground for pigeons.

An emergency assembly will meet today to decide who should lead the country.

For Fernando de la Rua, who resigned as president, the public's message has been clear: "Get out!"

Yesterday morning, as the Argentine parliament formally accepted his resignation, de la Rua offered no apologies for leaving Argentina in economic ruin.

Several successive pie charts filled the screen.

Today Argentina's economy is in free fall: Four in ten Argentines live in poverty, unemployment is near twenty per cent, the country owes $132 billion to foreign lenders and exports are down, as products are relatively expensive in other countries due to the peso being tied to the strong U.S. dollar.

The screen changed to show another park scene with SWAT-like police officers swarming everywhere. It took Marcela and Leonard a few seconds to realize what they were watching.

In other Buenos Aires news, a dramatic police takedown unfolded in a city park yesterday when Salvador Juárez, who was wanted for murdering a prison guard and a taxi driver during the 1972 Rawson Prison escape and several crimes since then - including kidnapping, extortion and rape - was apprehended after a shootout which left him and twenty-year-old Pedro Lopez with non-life-threatening gunshot wounds. Juárez was brought down, as he held a gun to the head of a teenage hostage, by a solid hit to the head from a wooden club swung by a visiting Canadian government bureaucrat, Frank Leonard. When Juárez turned his gun on Leonard, a nineteen-year police veteran fired a single shot from her revolver and hit Juárez in the arm, forcing him to drop the gun. He was immediately apprehended.

As he was being taken away, the semi-conscious Juárez claimed that he was a political prisoner.

———

Diego greeted Leonard with a handshake and a smile: "Well, the hero of the day!" He ignored Marcela.

"I think my part was blown out of proportion," Leonard replied. "The detective, Garcia, was the one who really saved the day."

Diego waved off the humility. "It took a lot of courage to do what you did."

"I think stupidity is a better word," Leonard laughed. "I'm just happy, thanks to Marcela and the police, everything worked out in the end."

"It looks like you took a pretty good hit to the head. Have you seen a doctor?"

"Yes. It's really nothing, probably won't even leave a scar. Marcela has taken great care of me."

Diego continued to ignore Marcela and any reference to her. "The media is all over this," he indicated the pile of newspapers on his desk. "I've already had several calls."

"Well, I definitely don't want to talk to any media," Leonard said. "I even refuse to talk to media on a wildfire."

"Don't worry, I'm going to direct all media requests to Marcela."

Marcela put up her hands in a defensive position, "Wait a minute," she protested. "I don't deal with the media either. We still have the report to finish and—"

She was cut off by the telephone ring.

Diego answered with his unhappy voice, "Mariana, I told you that we were not to be bothered." He listened for a moment, then, still unhappy he ordered "Send her away!" He listened to more on the other end. "Okay, I'll have Marcela come out to deal with it."

He hung up the phone and turned to Marcela. "You have your first customer," he told her. "Somebody is insisting on talking to our hero. Go deal with it."

"I'm not good at this," Marcela protested. "Can't Mariana deal with it?"

Diego was stone-faced. "Go!" he ordered.

After Marcela had reluctantly left the room, Leonard apologized. "Diego, I'm sorry for this mess. You certainly don't need something like this right now."

Diego waved him off again. "Don't worry about it. What do they say in North America? Shit happens."

"I want you to know that the whole mess was completely my doing," Leonard continued. "Marcela was on top of everything, all the time. I don't know where I would have ended up without her."

"I'm sure she'll tell me all about it later," Diego said, unimpressed.

"And I don't think we'll have any problem getting the report in by tomorrow."

"Yes," Diego agreed, "I guess that's the thing to focus on now."

The door to the office opened and Marcela entered the room with a stone-cold serious expression. Both Diego and Leonard immediately understood that something very traumatic had occurred. A dark-skinned woman wearing a grey and white nun's habit followed Marcela into the room. She also had a very serious face.

"Leonard," Marcela said, in a reverent tone suitable to her expression. "This is Sister Rosario."

Leonard looked at the nun. She looked like other nuns he had seen on the streets. But then he saw the expression on her face. She was holding back a flood of emotion. When their eyes met, Leonard knew. Immediately felt his heart fall through his chest. The shock of recognition almost threw him out of his chair. The years fell away.

"This is your sister, Leonard." Tears streamed down Marcela's face. "It's Rosie."

———

Leonard wanted to rise, to stand up, but his legs wouldn't obey. Staring at the nun, he could see Rosie's eyes. But he had also seen Rosie in a little girl's eyes the day before. Was his injury still making him crazy? He looked to Marcela for help.

She nodded, "It's her, Leonard."

He finally stood. He could only say, "I'm sorry, Rosie."

His sister covered the distance between them in a second and reached for him. He held her tightly to be sure that she was real. All his emotions, all his pain, made him cry for the first time since Rosie had disappeared. "I'm sorry, Rosie. I'm so sorry," was all he could utter.

The nun who was Rosie hugged him, patting his back and repeating, "*Está bien,* Lenny, *Está bien.*"

Marcela and Diego discreetly left the room.

Leonard finally had the strength to release his bear hug and take a step back. He held Rosie at arm's length and looked through the tears and deeply into her. This woman looked so old, so different on the outside - but he could see his sister clearly through her eyes.

"I see your photo in *el Dario*," she spoke in broken English. "Only *mi hermano* Lenny would use a stick to hit a man with gun." She smiled Rosie's radiant smile.

Leonard had so much to say, but all that would come out was, "I'm so sorry, Rosie."

She continued to smile, "*Por qué?*" she asked, "You have done *nada.*"

"I let him take you," Leonard whispered.

"What could you do? You were an eleven-year-old boy."

"I took Christine away."

"We have much to talk about. Right now, I have a commitment with the community kitchen. You will come to where I live tomorrow."

Leonard shook his head and squeezed her tightly again. "I don't want you to go. I've been looking for you for all of my life."

"*Está bien,*" she whispered in his ear. "I have many emotions right now. I need a little time. I promise I won't go away again."

When Leonard finally released his hold on her, Rosie took a paper and pen from Diego's desk and wrote down her address and phone number. She handed it to him.

He blurted out in a rush, "Forgive me, Rosie."

She put her warm hand on his wet cheek. "*Pobrecito,* you have done *nada. Tranquilo.*" She tilted up on her toes and kissed his forehead. "I'll see you tomorrow."

—

Marcela gave Diego the short version of what was going on in his office. He was as stunned as she was by the chain reaction of events that had led to Leonard being reunited with his sister after thirty-five years. Although he was definitely a cold-hearted government bureaucrat at the office, he too had a sister, and so he was not unaffected by the emotion of the situation. Marcela was surprised to see Diego's normally hard blue eyes go soft and wet.

Sister Rosario came out of his office first. She appeared more composed than Marcela expected her to be. "*Gracias, Señora,*" she said, as if Marcela had just passed her the salt at the dining room table. "I have left Lenny my address and phone number. If you could see that he makes it to my home tomorrow around noon, I would appreciate it."

Diego snapped out of his moment of sensitivity and put his arm around the nun and directed her towards the door "No problem, Sister. I have a driver attached to your brother. He'll be there at noon. Can I have him bring you anywhere now?"

"No, that won't be necessary. I don't have far to go." She slipped out quietly.

As Diego closed the door behind her, his office door opened again and Leonard appeared. Marcela noticed that he wasn't as composed as his sister had been. He looked shaken, and his eyes were red from crying. He gave them a weak smile, as if he had just lost someone close, rather than found someone. Marcela didn't know what to say.

"Are you okay?" she asked weakly.

"I'm still stunned," he confessed. "I can't believe what just happened." He looked at her for reassurance. "Did that just happen?"

Marcela smiled. "Yes, that did just happen." She approached him and took his arm. "What do you want to do now?"

"I guess I should phone, Christine. She's probably out of her mind with worry by now."

"Use my office," Diego offered.

After Leonard had left the room, Diego turned to Marcela. "You seem to have warmed up to your assignment. You know he only has one more day here?"

Marcela could only shrug. She couldn't think of anything to say. For the last few days she had been caught up in only the present moment. She hadn't thought beyond it. And she didn't want to think about it now.

Leonard was on the phone for only a few minutes. "She wasn't there," he said when he returned to the room. "I got the answering machine. I'll try again later."

CHAPTER ELEVEN

Marcela dropped the fire behaviour file on the kitchen table and sat down across from Leonard. He reached out and took the file, but she stopped him with her hand on his hand. "Let me do this," she said. "You've had quite a day and your head could use a rest. Why don't you relax in the other room?"

"No," Leonard insisted. "We'll work on this together. It will actually help me get my thinking straight."

Marcela pressed his hand softly. "What about your emotions? Don't you have to get them straight? Your life has changed today. It needs to settle."

"I *am* dealing with my emotions." Leonard grinned. "I'm giving them a rest. I'll need all my emotional strength when Rosie and I re-live the last thirty-five years."

Marcela frowned. "Just don't suppress any of these emotions. It's time to deal with them."

Leonard stared at her silently and squeezed her hand. Marcela felt her skin blush. She had meant the emotions of finding his long-lost sister. But he was stirring other emotions inside her. Emotions she wasn't so sure she wanted to confront.

"Okay," he said finally. "But how about I deal with them after we finish this report."

Marcela exhaled. "You're stubborn, Mr. Frank."

Using a draft of their predecessors' work, Marcela and Leonard completed the report in both Spanish and English in a couple of hours. It looked professional and contained all the buzzwords that bureaucrats like Diego would scan the document for. It certainly didn't merit the time and expense of a Canadian spending seven days in Argentina, but Marcela and Leonard knew that it wasn't about practicalities. This was about politics, budgets and bureaucracy. No one would ever read, or even refer, to the report, as it would contain nothing but obvious generalities and political niceties.

"Well, that went even faster than I thought it would," Leonard remarked looking at the printed versions in both languages.

"Yes," Marcela agreed. "Partly because we didn't come up with any profound revelations or any action items to be implemented. Just a pile of paper to show for the free vacations."

"It worked for me!" Leonard protested, with a smile.

"Oh!" Marcela put her hands to her mouth. "I didn't mean—"

Leonard laughed, "It's okay! I came here for personal reasons. It was a taxpayer-funded trip for me to fulfill a personal need, and now," he put his hand on the pile of paper, "I've fulfilled my commitment to the taxpayers."

"Well, it certainly did work for you." Marcela paused and then smiled. "And for me."

"Oh yes," Leonard said, missing the point. "Your daughter was almost killed, her boyfriend was shot and you have been stuck with babysitting me."

"That last part is what worked for me," Marcela replied, grinning.

Leonard thought for a second, and his eyes widened with realization. Suddenly, he became speechless.

Marcela laughed, "Come with me." She stood and offered her hand.

Leonard took her hand and stood up, still speechless. Was she taking him to her bedroom? Before he could get his mind up to speed, Marcela led him to the living room and put on a CD. "This is a good time to re-set yourself," she said and turned to him and with her arms in the dance position. "Let's tango," she said, and the music started.

When the phone rang, an hour later, Marcela had taught Leonard not only basic tango but how to perform it, complete with the requisite macho expression.

———

Leonard, left standing alone in the living room when Marcela went to the kitchen to answer the phone, closed his eyes and took a big breath. He felt warmth he had never felt before. He had found Rosie and she was alive and well. The cold burden that had frozen his soul for thirty-five years was released. He was surprised at feeling he could let her leave him again, but simply knowing she had survived was enough, for now. Tomorrow would be another day. He was a new man now; he could face the past. And he could look towards the future. The feeling he got from Marcela was good, the feeling when they moved their bodies together in a tango was good. Everything was different now.

———

June 1, 1965
Long Lake Indian Reserve
British Columbia, Canada

Rosie sat down at the table with Lenny and Christine and straightened her dress so that it looked pretty. All their friends and relatives were gathered in the Long Lake Community Hall for the wedding, and she wanted to look nice. Watching Uncle John get married to the French lady, Josette, had made her feel warm inside. Josette looked so beautiful in her white dress and with her flowing chestnut hair. And Uncle John looked like a Latin movie star, in his black suit and with his hair slicked back. Rosie couldn't help but picture herself in such a wedding.

Now the women were putting out the plates of smoked salmon, sliced moose roast and grouse stuffed with wild rice. Rosie's cousins, Walter and George, were tuning their guitar and fiddle. The fun was about to begin. She loved to watch her mother and father dance, they always seemed to be having so much fun.

Maybe she would be able to talk Lenny into dancing, and they could have fun too. But that was unlikely, Lenny was much too serious to dance and have fun. The wedding didn't seem to have the same warming effect on him. While she looked at the day as one in which she gained an auntie, Lenny looked at it as one in which he was losing his favourite uncle. He sat with his arms folded across his chest, clearly uncomfortable in his buttoned-up white shirt and stiff black shoes. He was wearing his I-don't-want-to-be-here expression.

Lenny loved to listen to Uncle's stories of fighting fire in the north, where he spent his summers on an all-Indian fire crew, and his escapades in the south, where he spent his winters and all his money. But that was all over now. Part of the deal for Josette to marry Uncle was that he took a full-time job at the asbestos mine in Cassiar, near the Yukon border, so they could have a home and a regular family life and he wouldn't be away all summer. She was French-Canadian Catholic, and children were in the future.

Christine, too, looked grumpy and out of place in her yellow chiffon dress and with her wild raven hair tied with a bow. Her expression plainly asked; Why can't we eat the cake now so I can get out of here? She wore a dress only because Josette had bribed her to wear it by offering her the biggest and best piece of the wedding cake.

Walter's guitar was tuned and George's bow was rosined, and they went right into "The Tennessee Waltz." Everyone turned to the bride and groom and started clapping hands. Uncle stood there with his hands out, asking "What?" Josette elbowed him and put her arms out in a dancing position. Rosie put her hand to her mouth to hide her giggle. Finally Uncle "got it" and, with an embarrassed, boyish look, took hold of Josette and proceeded to glide her through a perfect waltz. Rosie's mother dragged her father out to the dance floor where they proceeded to stumble through a not-so-perfect waltz. Soon all the couples were dancing, and Rosie caught Lenny's eye. He rolled his eyes and mouthed, "Forget it."

When the song was over, everyone clapped and laughed, and then spread out and mingled while the boys discussed their next song and had a drink of punch. There was no alcohol allowed in the hall, which meant that there would be no fights. No doubt a few cousins were out in the back with a bottle, and there was bound to be a few altercations with them, but Rosie was sure this was going to be all fun.

Uncle John and Josette, now Auntie Josette, were making the rounds with handshakes and kisses, and Rosie was thrilled to see them approach her. "You look beautiful!" Josette exclaimed.

"I'd say she's the second most beautiful woman here," Uncle John agreed.

"Thank you," Rosie giggled, embarrassed and pleased.

Looking at Lenny, Uncle John said, "And you look a little serious there, partner."

Lenny responded with an indifferent shrug.

"When do I get my cake?" Christine asked her new auntie.

"Gee, Christine," Lenny spoke up, "how rude. Can't you wait?"

"No," Josette cut in, "It's okay. I promised. And don't you look pretty in that dress, Christine. Aren't you glad you wore it?"

"No, I feel stupid," Christine grumbled.

Lenny laughed for the first time. "You look like Auntie Mabel's ugly dog when she dressed it up for Christmas."

Even Christine couldn't help but laugh, remembering how stupid and out of place the rat-like Chihuahua looked with the little green dress wrapped around his tiny body and the set of red reindeer antlers clipped to his boney head. Everyone in Auntie Mable's house couldn't help but laugh at the time either. It was the last time Father's entire family had all been together. After that Christmas, a year and a half ago, everyone seemed to either spread out or die. Grandpa and Grandma both went with tuberculosis, John went firefighting and traveling, Mabel and her family moved to Vancouver, and Marie, the oldest sibling, hanged herself on Easter Day. Nobody could, or would, tell Rosie why. Her father was the only one of the family who didn't move off the reserve, and he managed to stay alive.

"Come on, Johnny," Josette took her new husband's arm. "I think it's time to cut the cake." She turned to Christine, "You can have your piece after we take photographs."

As Uncle John and Josette strolled off across the wooden floor to the cake table, Roger and Clem, twelve year old identical twin boys, came and sat down at their table. Rosie usually kept her distance from the twins because they usually meant trouble. She had heard that Roger had already got drunk once. But then, the twins' father was always drunk, and he beat them regularly.

Roger spoke first. "This is pretty boring."

"The wedding was stupid," Clem added.

"I liked it," Rosie said.

"You would," Clem sneered. "You're a girl."

Roger turned to Lenny. "I hear they're taking more kids to that school."

Lenny shrugged. "So what? I'm not going."

"I don't think they're asking," Roger said. "I think you have to go."

"I think it might be nice," Rosie said. "It's not like you go forever. And you learn to read and write and play sports. It could be fun."

"No," Roger disagreed, "I shot my first moose last week. That was fun."

Rosie wasn't about to argue. "Well, I'm going to watch them cut the cake."

Christine was off her chair immediately, "I'm going to eat the cake."

———

Christine looked around the airport terminal while her call went through and remembered why she hated LAX. It was terribly organized, had no character and the people were generally disgruntled and unhelpful. It was such a contrast for anyone coming from the Vancouver airport, which was well organized, full of amazing Native art and serviced with elderly volunteers wearing green jackets who could tell you whatever you needed to know about the airport or the city. It was a good thing she had a three hour hold-over in L.A., as it would take her at least two hours to get through the smelly maze and gauntlet of security to the other terminal.

She had just enough extra time to get an international phone card and attempt to phone the number Marcela had given her. The phone rang several times. Just when she was ready to hang up, a voice answered, *"Hola."*

"Marcela?"

"Si, es Marcela."

"It's Christine, Leonard's sister. Have you found out anything about Leonard?"

"Christine! Yes, he's here right now. I'll get him."

"Hold on, Marcela. Is he all right?"

"Yes, don't worry! He's fine."

"Shit. No, I mean that's great! But I got a little freaked out after I talked to you, and now I'm on my way to Buenos Aires. I probably should have waited for your next call, but I was worried. Now all of a sudden it doesn't seem like such a good idea - leaving Leonard's house unwatched and using his money for the plane ticket."

"No, Christine, I'm sure he won't mind. Let me get him."

"No, don't. Let me surprise him. How do I get to where you are from the Buenos Aires airport? I get there at 1:30 tomorrow afternoon."

"Perfect timing. I'll pick you up."

"Great! I'll be the young and beautiful girl dressed in tight jeans and great boobs."

Marcela smiled. "I think I'll be able to pick you out of the crowd."

"Okay, Leonard told you: Middle-aged, plain looking, dressed like a hippie and sadly real boobs."

"We must be twins!"

"Do you like my brother, Marcela? Because you sound like someone I could get along with, and Lenny usually goes more for the stupid and boring type."

"Your brother has gone through a few changes since you last saw him."

"I hope compassion for his little sister is one of them."

"I'm not sure, but my guess is he has gained some compassion."

"I'd better go now. Have to make my way through this shit hole to my next gate. Thanks, Marcela."

"*Hasta mañana*, Christine."

Christine put the phone back in its cradle and tried to gather her thoughts. Leonard was fine. Everything was a big misunderstanding. She had taken three thousand dollars from his secret Player's Tobacco tin that he had hidden underneath the floorboards in the bedroom, and flown to the other side of the earth. All for a misunderstanding! It seemed like the obvious thing to do, at the time; but in retrospect, she thought maybe she had acted hastily.

But there was no turning back now. She would have to pay him back. Someday.

Might as well call it a holiday and have fun.

———

Marcela, smiling, hung up the phone. It was good to be involved in this monumental family reunion. She wasn't entirely happy that she had to keep Christine's arrival a secret, but it would be a nice secret.

And she wanted so badly to tell Christine about Sister Rosario, but that pleasure should be reserved for Leonard. She shivered with excitement, then wiped the smile from her face and tucked her secrets away. She returned to the living room.

Leonard remained standing where she left him at mid-tango to answer the phone. But he looked different, somehow. She could not think of a time that she had ever seen a man more content.

———

Olivia arrived back at the apartment at the latest minute her mother had allowed, the stroke of midnight. This was two hours later than her usual curfew, but since she was only at the hospital with Pedro, her mother loosened the reins. She entered quietly, even knowing that the next morning her mother would know the exact second she had arrived. The apartment was silent and the lights were out, but candlelight flickered from the living room. Peeking in, Olivia saw her mother cuddled up with Leonard on the couch. Both were sound asleep.

Olivia smiled and remained in the doorway looking at them. It was the first time she had ever seen her mother with a man. Her mother had never seriously dated anyone in Olivia's entire life; Marcela's time had been dedicated to her work and to her daughter. Perhaps, now, her mother would see things differently. Maybe she would fall in love again. Olivia blew out the candle and tiptoed to bed, content that her boyfriend's wounds would heal and her mother's pain from the past might finally evaporate.

—

June 28, 1982
El Bolsón, Argentina

Abuelo Marcelo rocked back and forth in his rocking chair, staring in the direction of the mountain - Piltriquitron. If there was a dimensional door lost in one of those rocky crevasses, he wanted to pass through it. Hopefully the other dimension would be free of pain and suffering, because this dimension had more than its share. Marcelo wanted to cry out so many times and point his finger. He wanted to blame someone, or something, for all the misfortune and heartbreak in his life. The Argentine military government was the obvious target. Its ruthlessness and stupidity brought so much hardship and difficulty to the Argentine man and so much anguish to the Argentine woman. It cut the country apart with knives of idiocy and created wounds that might never heal. Lives and families had been destroyed. Marcelo hoped that they would all burn in hell.

His heart was sinking to a new low. His seventeen-year-old granddaughter was lying in her bedroom with only one reason to go on living - the human life inside her. What words could he say to her to make her feel any different? They had taken both of her parents and now the father of her baby. How was a man supposed to console a girl who had lost that much for reasons so unreasonable? She needed more than the comfort he could provide. She needed purpose, and hope in the future. Marcelo's only purpose was her, and his only hope for the future was the baby she carried.

The baby is definitely a blessing. A godsend!

It would be his granddaughter's reason for living.

It occurred to Marcelo that he had passed through a metaphorical door to another dimension in life. He made a vow to himself as he rocked back and forth staring at the mountain. He would pray every day to the Virgin. He would take shamanic journeys every month. He would perform every healing technique his spirit animal, the Cougar, would advise. He would do everything humanly and spiritually possible, until the life inside his granddaughter emerged. After the baby was born, he would dedicate the rest of his years and his meagre wealth to his last two loved ones. Together they would break the chain of tragedy and start anew.

But first things first. Right now, Marcelita was a grieving, pregnant teenage widow with no mother or father. She needed to be convinced that there was a future for her and her child.

CHAPTER ELEVEN

Day Six
December 23, 2001

Leonard's joy had not diminished overnight. These had been the most emotionally packed twenty-four hours of his life. Things could never be more powerful than they were now. He and Marcela sat together in the back seat, as Ernesto drove according to Marcela's orders - at a respectable speed, with no music of any kind. And Leonard sat in silence, enveloped in warmth as Marcela held his hand.

Ernesto was familiar with the area where Sister Rosario lived and had no problem finding the address. He pulled into the driveway of a large, white two-storey building with a red tile roof and black iron railings along the balconies. Several children kicked a ball on an expansive green lawn, and a few nuns manicured the colourful gardens surrounding the estate. Leonard had seen this scene before, in his imagination. It was his fantasy residential school.

Marcela patted Leonard's knee. "Here you are, Leonard. It looks like your sister lives in a tranquil place."

Leonard smiled. "Yes," he agreed, "that's exactly what I was thinking." He turned to Marcela. "Thank you for everything." A fake cough came from their driver. Leonard laughed. "And thank you too, Ernesto. I wouldn't be sitting here in Rosie's driveway without either of you."

Marcela smiled and then kissed his cheek. "*No hay problema.* Now go visit with your sister. Ernesto and I have some things to do that will take a couple of hours. We'll come back and see you when we finish."

Leonard stepped out of the car and took a deep breath.

Rosie had appeared at the front door. She was wearing her white and grey habit and a bright smile. Leonard followed the red brick walkway towards her, feeling as if he were floating. They came together and hugged each other tightly. Leonard closed his eyes and savoured the moment.

Rosie pulled back. "*Vamos adentro.* I have tea ready."

Leonard followed her into the house, or whatever it was - a mansion, or a convent, perhaps an orphanage. He looked around the spacious entry room and saw the elaborate detail in every piece of trim and doorway. No expense had been spared, Leonard mused, but it was not-over-the-top lavish. Several landscape paintings donned the walls and the furniture was old, but not ragged. The place felt comfortable.

"This is quite the house," he remarked.

"Let's sit down in the sun room and talk," Rosie said. "I'll get the tea."

The sun room was a second-floor room that extended to a balcony and overlooked the estate vegetable garden. Large windows provided sunlight for the jungle of house plants and the sitting area. Leonard and Rosie sat at a small round table that held a porcelain tea pot, two teacups and a plate of chocolate chip cookies.

Rosie slid the plate closer to Leonard. "I remembered you loved these cookies baked in our wood stove."

Leonard took one and looked at it. He smiled; it was a cookie from his past, a cookie that had been buried deep in his subconscious. It was warm and exactly like he remembered. "And you would give me half your share," he reminded her.

Rosie smiled. "Yes, and Christine would steal the other half." She paused as they both remembered. "How is Christine?" she asked, with some hesitation.

Leonard laughed with his mouth full. "Exactly the same pain in the ass she always was." He took a drink of tea. "She's never married, but then she hasn't been alone much either. She lied her way into a job with the local newspaper, and it has actually lasted a couple of years.

She's pretty good at it. We both live north of Long Lake, in Smithers and I work for the Ministry of Forests as a fire behaviour specialist. I've never married, either."

Rosie stared at him with a blank face. "Lenny," she said, "May I ask you to speak more slowly? I haven't spoken in English for years."

"Oh, I'm sorry." It suddenly occurred to Leonard that a lot had changed. He wasn't only talking to his sister; he was talking to Sister Rosario and should be respectful of her.

"And Mother and Father?" she asked.

Leonard's expression froze. In all of his bliss, he had never considered that at some point he would have to tell Rosie the fate of their mother and father. He had buried the memory long ago, and had no intention of ever digging it back up. Their fates were resting in a Pandora's box of guilt, anger and hate. Although Leonard and Christine had talked occasionally about their parents, they had never spoken of their deaths.

———

Christmas Day 1965
Long Lake Indian Reserve
British Columbia, Canada

Peter Frank stared at the twenty-six-ounce bottle of Canadian Club rye whisky as if he were trying to levitate it. Actually, he wanted it to disappear. He was not a drinker, he was a bush Indian who just wanted to raise a family and be left alone. He had a traditional trapline where he could make a few dollars and the hunters he guided tipped him good if they were able to shoot something. Sadie tanned moose and caribou hides and made moccasins to sell to the hunters. The children loved the life of the elders and were eager to learn it all. No one could do bead work like Rosie. Lenny had shot his first moose at the age of ten. Christine started making snowshoes by herself at the age of eight. Then, four months ago, on August 10, 1965, it had been all taken away. The priest had walked into their cabin with a baby-faced member of the Royal Canadian Mounted Police and had simply taken the children away. The priest said they needed to be taught things to help them survive in the modern world that Peter couldn't teach them. Sadie, protesting with painful screams, had cried out like a wounded bear. The cop had to hold her back. Lenny refused to go and Christine had bitten the priest. It was a chaotic scene of screaming and yelling and flailing bodies; only Rosie went quietly and gracefully. Peter just sat through it all, staring in disbelief, until the dust from the priest's station wagon had settled and Sadie was crying on the ground, pounding the dirt with her fists, and their three children were gone. And they would not be coming back any time soon. Peter had no choice but to go and get them. This bothered him a great deal, because he didn't operate well in a white environment. There were too many rules for Indians, too many dangerous people.

The cabin door creaked open and a rush of the minus forty degree air collided with the warmth of the cabin. Sadie shuffled in through the steam. She had not changed the filthy cotton pants or the Toronto Maple Leafs t-shirt that she had worn that day, nor had she bathed. She had burnt off her long shiny black hair into a short uneven mess resembled the tail of a porcupine. In four months, Peter's beautiful wife had become a devastated wreck.

She dropped herself in the chair across from him. She had asked her cousin for the bottle of whisky, so they could have a Christmas drink for the children. "Are you going to just stare at that bottle, or are we going to have a Christmas drink?"

Peter had seen enough to know that drinking whisky never ended quietly or peacefully, but he couldn't deny Sadie this solace. She needed an escape, a distraction. And although he hated to admit it, Peter needed it too. He needed it to help find the courage to bring his children home.

He twisted off the cap of the bottle and threw the cap into the firewood box. He poured a drink for his wife and another for himself. They looked at each other for a few seconds. Then Sadie put the glass to her lips and tipped it back. She set the glass down with an expression of pain tightening the skin of her face.

Peter gulped down his drink and the fire seared the inside of his throat down to his stomach. He kept a straight face, even though all his muscles were contracting and twisting. He poured another glass for each of them.

He kept pouring until the bottle was done.

The frigid air coming in through the open door brought Peter back. He was still sitting at the table behind the empty whisky bottle. He wiped the saliva off his chin and squinted to see through the blur. Sadie was gone, probably in the outhouse, and she had left the fucking door open. He stood up on shaky legs, steadying himself with a hand on the table. He made his way to the door, but when he went to close it, he saw his wife lying face down in the snow. He cried out her name and ran to her. Her body was frozen rigid. He turned her over and saw her skin had turned blue. Vomit was frozen to her face. He didn't cry. He picked her up and carried her to their bed. He laid her down gently and tucked her in with the quilt she had made when she was pregnant with Rosie. He kissed her frozen lips and smiled sadly at her. She was still beautiful to him. "I'm sorry, my love," he apologized out loud. "I'm sorry I failed you and the kids. You deserved better." He went to the door and took his loaded 30/30 Winchester rifle from its place - the rifle his father had given him and he had planned to pass on to Lenny — and switched off the safety. Then he sat on the bed and looked down at his wife one more time. The only woman he ever loved. Tears began to run freely down his face. Without hesitating or thinking, he stood the rifle up between his feet with the butt on the floor, leaned over and pressed the barrel against his destroyed heart, and pulled the trigger.

——

Rosie listened quietly with her hands together on her lap. When Leonard finished, her eyes were wet and her lips quivered slightly. "So much pain and suffering were caused by those schools," she said. "I'm happy that you and Christine survived."

Leonard shook his head. "You are the survivor, Rosie."

There was a silent reflective moment for both, and then Leonard continued. "It wasn't easy," he said, speaking slowly and simply so that his sister could follow and understand. "When you disappeared from the school, I felt that I had failed you, that I didn't protect you. I knew that I had to get Christine out before she disappeared too. I also knew that I had to get myself out, before Father Ricardo beat me to death. One night, not long after you disappeared, I snuck out of my dorm and eventually found Christine in her bed. We were nearly caught, several times, but we eventually made our way north until Uncle John and Auntie Josette found us in Prince George. They told us about Mother and Father." Leonard took a deep breath. "And they took us home with them to Cassiar. That was the mining town they'd moved to after they got married. Turned out they couldn't have children, so we became their children. It worked out good for everyone. Auntie Josette did home schooling for both Christine and me, and Uncle showed us how to work and get along in the world." Leonard stopped and thought. "They accomplished what the residential school never could. They taught us to be white."

——

April 23, 1972
Cassiar, British Columbia, Canada

Lenny was certain of only a few things in life after his first eighteen years. One of them was that he was not going to work at the asbestos mine all of his life. It wasn't that he didn't respect the work, or that he was too good for it; he just didn't like it. He wanted to be in the mountains, in the bush, where he felt the best, not in the mill sweeping up asbestos dust or operating equipment in the asbestos pit at the top of the mountain, enduring harsh winter conditions and surviving dangerous switchbacks. It was honest work, but there was other honest work.

Lenny heard about a job fighting forest fires for the summer from Leo Marelli, the goalie on his hockey team and the son of the mine manager. Lenny liked Leo: Leo offered up passionate Italian drama for every topic and he pushed Lenny to get out in the world and have fun.

"No fuckin' way I'm going to follow in my old man's fuckin' footsteps," he said on Saturday as they laced up their skates. *"I'm going up to the forestry base in Lower Post on Monday. I heard they had some openings for firefighters. They're training some new special crew that rappel on ropes from fuckin' helicopters into the fire and build pads so that the helicopters can land and fight the fire. That's what I want to do. Not only is it exciting, but you probably get the chicks with a job like that. And it only*

lasts the summer! Then I go on unemployment insurance and winter in fuckin' Mexico."

Lenny understood the logic and was immediately intrigued. *"That sounds pretty good."* He wanted to say *"fuckin' good,"* but he just couldn't bring himself to say swear words. Auntie Josette had a rule about swearing, and even Christine had eventually learned to follow Auntie's rules.

Number One Rule: Be respectful. This includes no swearing and no arguing with adults.

Number Two Rule: Tell the truth. Always!

Number Three Rule: Be diligent with school work.

Lenny had no problem with the first two rules; the problem was number three. Auntie insisted on six hours of school work a day, five days a week, and it took Lenny a few weeks of washing dishes to get on to the third rule. Christine, on the other hand, seemed to have no problem at all with spending her days doing school work. She did, however, have a problem learning the first two rules.

"You should come with me!" Leo blurted out, as if it were a profound realization. *"Maybe we can both get on. That would be so fuckin' cool!"*

Lenny agreed to go along with Leo, but he had reservations. He didn't want to screw up Leo's chance at a job. Maybe Leo didn't see Lenny as Indian, but most people did - they were raised in a racist culture and prejudged every Indian as stupid, and there wasn't much you could do about it. The racism was too prevalent and ingrained for any one person to change minds. Lenny only had to watch television and read newspapers to understand that. In a way, racism worked in Lenny's favour: his narrow eyes, black hair and solid build made some whites think he was Asian and, therefore, smarter than the average white. He played that card as long as he could, even developing a decent nondescript accent.

But he wouldn't play games with this opportunity Leo was offering. It was something he was sure he could do, and do well. He knew that to fight wildfire, a person had to be in good physical shape, smart on his feet, at home in the bush and aware of the weather. Lenny was confident that he was that guy. He would just be himself.

On Monday morning, Lenny waited impatiently for Leo. He got to his feet and looked out the window whenever he heard a vehicle, which was about every fifteen seconds, as people were going to work at that time of morning.

"You seem a little nervous, Lenny," Uncle noticed. "What's up?"

"Oh, it's nothing. Leo's picking me up and we're going to Lower Post to see about a job."

"What kind of job would you find in Lower Post?" his uncle asked with a slight laugh. "It's a Kaska reserve, and you're not Kaska."

"Leo says there's a government forestry base there and they're going to hire some people for fighting forest fires."

"Well, I did that for a few years on a crew out of Prince George. Maybe I could talk to some people I know down there. But you're eighteen now, I can get you on with the company, which will pay a lot more than fighting fires."

"Thanks Uncle, but this is a special thing. They're going to train guys to repel from helicopters."

Uncle started to say something, and then stopped and looked thoughtful for a couple of seconds, "Well," he said finally, "it sounds interesting. Good luck with it."

Uncle John always emphasized that Lenny and Christine should take control of their own lives and do whatever they wanted. Sure, he acknowledged, it might be more difficult, being Native (Uncle John was the first person Lenny heard use the word "Native" rather than Indian), but that just means there would be a few more hurdles to jump. Lenny and Christine would just have to jump higher and faster than a white person.

Christine had entered the living room and overheard the job description. "That sounds like a cool job, I want to do that too," she said casually. "Where do we sign up?"

"You can't do it," Lenny scoffed. "You're a girl and you're only sixteen. They want strong men."

"Well, that leaves you out."

Lenny heard a vehicle and looked out the window. Leo had pulled up in his father's Ford truck. "We'll see," he said.

Christine looked out and saw Leo sitting in the driver's seat. "You're going with that dolt?" She shook her head. "At least he'll make you look smart."

The drive to Lower Post from Cassiar took about an hour and a half, crossing over the Yukon border then dipping back into British Columbia along the Liard River, which was just enough time for Leo to drink a few beers and smoke a couple of joints. Lenny refused both. He never drank alcohol out of respect for the death of his parents, and he didn't think smoking a joint was the best way to prepare for applying for a job. He had smoked pot several times and he kind of liked the high, but not enough to buy his own and smoke it regularly. And he certainly didn't want to disappoint Uncle and Auntie, who were both vehemently anti-drugs of any kind.

By the time Leo turned off the Alaska Highway onto the access road to Lower Post, his eyes were red and he was grinning stupidly at nothing. They passed several log cabins and spotted a couple of teenage girls walking along the road.

"Check them out," Leo slurred. "Let's ask them where the forest ranger dude is."

"Okay," Lenny said. "Pull up to them and I'll ask."

"Oh, I get it, because you're Indian, uh, I mean Native and they're Native, you get to do all the talking."

"No, it's because you're an idiot and I'm not."

"Fuck you."

The girls turned out to be barely teenagers and gave directions to the forest ranger's building in incomprehensible giggles, but since there were only a couple of streets to Lower Post, it only took a few minutes to find. Just another one of the log buildings, but it had the British Columbia government insignia on the door.

Lenny knocked on the door rather than walking right in. A gruff voice snapped, "Yeah, come in. The door isn't locked."

Lenny walked in first, with Leo stumbling in behind him, tripping on the door sill and pushing Lenny into the centre of the room.

"What the hell are you guys looking for?" The forest ranger was sitting casually on his desk shaking his head.

"A job!" Leo blurted out. "We wanna jump out of fuckin' helicopters."

The ranger smiled and turned to pick up some papers on his desk. "Here's the application," he handed a paper to each of them. "Fill these out and we'll see what happens, but the rappel program won't be off the ground for a couple more years."

The ranger didn't seem like too much of a hardass, so Lenny decided to be a little bold. He stepped out and offered a handshake. "My name is Lenny Frank, sir."

The ranger slipped off the desk and shook Lenny's hand. "Glad to meet you Lenny. I'm the ranger here. Jim Westby." He offered his hand to Leo as well, catching him a bit off guard.

"Oh yeah, I'm Leo." He shook the ranger's hand too enthusiastically. "Do you have a bathroom? I have to piss like a racehorse."

"There's an outhouse in the back."

Leo hurried out the door and left Lenny standing with the ranger.

"Mr. Westby, is there anything more I can do than just fill out the application to get noticed? I'm really interested in forest fire work. I'm sure that I could do a good job." And then he added, just so that would be no doubt, "I don't drink, sir."

"I have one initial attack position open. Our season starts in two weeks. Be here on that Monday, at eight a.m." The ranger looked Lenny directly in the eye. "Bring your work boots and lose your friend. You'll have to pass a physical fitness test and a written test on basic firefighting. You'll also be required to get your first-aid ticket."

"Thank you, sir. I'll be there."

"Don't disappoint me, son."

Lenny didn't disappoint Jim Westby that Monday - or at any other time in their twenty- five-year relationship. Jim became Lenny's mentor and close friend and was the sole reason that Lenny was able to rise to the top, to become the province's most respected expert on fire behaviour. If a large fire was threatening, then Leonard Frank was the one to get.

———

Leonard and Rosie reached for their teacups at the same time and sipped in silence. Leonard took another cookie and looked at it before he took a bite. "And what about you?" he asked her, as if inquiring about her day.

"Me?" Rosie smiled nervously and put her teacup on the table, as it began to shake in her hand, sending ripples along the surface of the tea. "I don't know where to start." She took a minute to compose herself. "Sisters Catalina, Elisa and I operate this estate as a shelter for children. We provide a safe place, some meals and some counselling."

"I need to hear what happened to you from the day we arrived at the residential school until now." Leonard was looking at Rosie intensely. "You can give me the short version, but please don't leave out any key parts. The best time in my life to hear this is right now, and I don't want to pass it up."

Rosie's tightened face suddenly relaxed. She pointed out the window, to Ernesto pulling into the brick-lined driveway. "Look, your friends are back."

"This isn't going to save you from telling the story," Leonard said as he watched Marcela get out of the car. "I need to—" he stopped talking and his eyes widened. "My God!" he said finally. "I don't believe it."

"What?" Rosie asked, looking down at the people getting out of the car. "What's wrong?"

Marcela spotted them in the window and waved. Leonard waved back and shook his head. A woman stepped up next to Marcela and also waved with a big smile.

Rosie grasped her brother's hand to steady herself.

Leonard held her firm. "It looks like someone else will be sitting in on your story." He pointed down to the car. "That's your little sister, Christine."

—

Christine stuck a smile on her face and waved to Lenny and the nun in the window, but from the corner of her mouth she said to Marcela, "Okay, I get it. Lenny *has* changed. He's a reborn Catholic." She continued to wave. "Shit, it's worse than I thought."

"It's not that bad," Marcela assured her with a grin.

"Not you too!" She turned to Marcela. "It's a good thing I came. Somebody here has to represent the dark side."

"Come on," Marcela said as she took Christine's arm. "Let's go inside, so that you can also see the light."

They were met at the door by another nun, who silently greeted them and led them through the entry room and up the stairway. Christine scanned the expansive room and high ceilings and she ran her fingers over the hand carved railing that curved around with the stairway.

"Jesus Christ," she exclaimed under her breath. "Is this the fucking pope's house?" The nun leading them hesitated and turned her head slightly. Marcela put a finger to her lips, the international sign language for "Shut up, idiot" and pointed to the nun. Christine understood and covered her mouth with her hand, the sign language for "Shit, I'm an idiot."

At the top of the stairs the nun opened the door and, with a sweep of the arm, directed them inside. As Christine walked passed her, the nun gave her a stern look. Christine smiled back; she wasn't fond of nuns and she could not have cared less what any nun thought about her. Inside the room, the air was scented by the many plants that soaked in the sunlight streaming in through the large, open windows. Leonard was standing with his arm around the nun, the stupidest smile ever on his face and a large bruise in the centre of his forehead. Christine was surprised that he didn't come to her with one of his bear hugs. But he stayed with the nun, holding the stupid smile.

"Well Lenny, you're okay," Christine said, uncomfortably. "Praise the Lord!"

"Christine," Leonard said through his smile, "I would like you to meet Sister Rosario."

Christine looked past the nun's habit and at her face. The nun smiled and Christine smiled back. There was something familiar. The shape of the mouth. The friendly brown eyes. The warmth of her presence.

Then Christine knew.

The floor began to give way and Marcela was steadying her. Then, the nun who was her sister came and wrapped Christine in her arms. Great, heaving sobs erupted, more joy than either could control. Christine had not cried since she and Leonard had escaped the residential school. Not even when she learned of her parent's fate. She had become emotionally untouchable. But now, she let it all out and cried uncontrollably.

"Okay," Leonard said after five minutes of both his sisters bawling. "I didn't even cry that much."

Christine turned and looked at him with her eyes red and wet. "Go to hell," she said and then remembered that she was hugging a nun. "Oh, sorry," she said to Rosie and then hugged her tightly again. "Where have you been, sister of mine? What happened to you?"

"She was about to tell me," Leonard interjected, "when you showed up and started snivelling like a baby." He winked at Marcela.

Marcela also had tears in her eyes. "I'm going to leave you alone together for a while," she said. "You have Ernesto's cell number. Give us a call when you want to be picked up."

"You knew Christine was coming," Leonard said, smiling at her. "Did you have something to do with this?

Marcela shook her head in defence. "I only found out last night, when she was already on her way. She asked me not to tell you. And I didn't tell her about Rosie. I'm just a victim of circumstance."

Leonard walked her to the front door. "Marcela, I don't know how to thank you. I'm piling up a pretty big debt to you."

She turned to him and put both her hands on his face. "You've given me *mucho*," she said, gazing in his eyes. Then, in an almost involuntary motion, they kissed each other slowly on the lips. When their lips pulled away, Marcela was still holding Leonard's face. "I'll be waiting for your call," she said. "Enjoy this moment with your family."

━━━

Rosie, Christine and Leonard, having finally dried their tears and slowed their heartbeats, settled in three chairs around the table in the sunroom. The other nun brought in more tea and chocolate chip cookies, and Rosie introduced her as Sister Catalina.

"I am very happy for you," Sister Catalina said, with both hands on her heart. "You have been blessed." She was looking at Christine, who was rolling her eyes into the teenager-perfected "Yeah, whatever" expression.

"So, Christine," Leonard started in, briefing her just as he briefed new reinforcements on fires. "I've given Rosie—" he paused. "Should we call you Rosie or Sister Rosario, or just Rose?"

Rosie smiled, "You're my brother, Lenny."

Leonard nodded. "Okay, I've given Rosie a breakdown of our last thirty-five years." His voice became serious. "I've also told her about Mother and Father."

"Holy shit!" Christine yelped. "These are exactly like the cookies Mom used to bake." She snatched one up and inspected it closely. "Exactly!"

"Christine." Leonard was waving his hands to get her attention, and Rosie was holding her hands to her mouth to hide her giggling. "Please pay attention. And Spanish is Rosie's first language now, so speak slowly and, for once, think about what you say."

"I'm listening," she protested through a mouthful of cookie. "You told her a bunch of lies, which probably put you in a good light and made me look like a harebrained slut." She stopped and put her hand to her mouth and said, "Please don't tell me that you told her about my seven abortions!" She laughed and reached for her sister's hand. "I'm just joking, Rosie. You'll get used to me."

Rosie's giggles turned to a laugh. "You haven't changed a bit," she said when she stopped laughing.

"That's for sure," Leonard said. "I bet she's thinking right now how to steal your share of the cookies."

"I don't know what you're talking about," Christine said innocently. "I've never had more than my fair share."

"Yes," Leonard shot back, "but what you consider fair share and what is actually fair are two different things."

"Maybe only different in your reality."

"Hey!" Rosie suddenly cut in. "Stop your bickering or I'll take the cookies and feed them to the dog."

All three burst out laughing. Laughing so hard their sides hurt, like they hadn't laughed since they were children.

Leonard caught his breath first. "Man, that was a blast from the past."

"I'll bet that neither of you knew that I baked those cookies most of the time," Rosie said. "I was the one that made them that shape. Mother was too busy making bread, drying meat and doing the million other things she had to do. She had no time to make cookies! She showed me how to do it with a couple of batches, and I put it into my routine. I was a very organized little girl. You two were always all over the place and never paid attention to anything. You saw cookies and didn't question where they came from, you would instantly fight over where they were going and dividing them into shares, as you both just did."

Both Leonard and Christine shifted uncomfortably in their chairs.

Rosie smiled. "Of course, because you just assume that Mom made them, you couldn't know that I had secured my share before they even reached your greedy little fingers."

Christine clapped her hands together. "The truth finally comes out!" she laughed.

"And there's more to tell," Leonard added. His sisters lost their smiles and turned to him. "I only have one more day here in Argentina," he pleaded. "I really have to know what I have spent most of my life searching for but could never find. I need to know what happened to you at the school and what happened after you were taken away."

"Maybe she doesn't want to tell you," Christine chirped.

"No, it's all right," Rosie said. "You both have the right to know. She took a sip from her tea and folded her hands together on her lap. "It started the day after we arrived at the school," she began in a once-upon-a-time voice.

—

Rosie wasn't entirely against the idea of the residential school when her cousin, Sandy Tom, first told her that a priest was taking all the children to a school where they would live away from their parents, but able to come home on some holidays. They would learn how to speak English, how to read and write, and how to behave properly. And Sandy had heard from the priest himself that they gave children lollipops. Rosie loved her parents and was sure that she already knew how to behave properly, but she did want to learn more English and read books. And she wasn't averse to receiving a lollipop, or two.

It didn't take long for her first impression to change. She soon wished she had never heard of residential school. Her doubts started with the harsh separation from their mother and father. The policeman should have never pushed her mother to the ground and left her screaming. The entire six hours in the car with Father Ricardo, they were not allowed to speak. Both Leonard and Christine did speak though, and were promptly slapped in the face with a willow stick, which the priest kept constantly in his grip even when he was driving. Rosie didn't make a sound. She was too scared to even move and she had to pee badly for the last two hours of the trip.

When they arrived at the school, Father Ricardo and a nun took all three children into a room. Without a word, the nun cut Rosie's hair into a bowl shape and doused her with some kind of powder to kill lice. Then, before Rosie could even clear the powder from her eyes, the nun was taking all of her clothes off and pushing her into a scalding hot shower. The water seared her young skin like red-hot needles. She screamed, but only inside herself, to avoid punishment. At least, she could finally pee. Leonard and Christine followed her through the same process but with more protest, which only got them another slap with the priest's willow stick. After the shower, they were all brought to stand naked, shivering and under the dark gaze of Father Ricardo. Finally, the nun arrived with the clothes that they would always wear.

Once they were all dressed in their blue trousers and had their white shirts tucked in, Father Ricardo had the nun take a picture of him with the three children. Finally, Rosie realized that her long, beautiful, shiny black braid had been cut and that the clothes her mother had made had been taken away. After the picture was taken, Leonard's little fist came out of nowhere and hit the priest in the chin. The priest knocked Leonard to the ground with the back of his hand and, taking him by the wrist, beat his hand with the willow until his fingers bled. Leonard refused to cry. The priest laughed, "Welcome to Saint Mary's. I'm sure that you and I will see much of each other. I'm looking forward to it. I'll make sure you get a copy of the photo so that you'll always have something to remember us by - all together, a happy family." He laughed again and slapped the willow against his leg.

Three younger nuns came and took the three children away to three separate dormitories. The boys' area was separated from the girls' area with a wire fence. The girls were separated by age: under twelve years old and over twelve. Rosie finally spoke, protesting to the nun that Christine and she had slept together all their lives and it would be better for them to be together now. The nun, Sister Bernadette, was very nice and said that she would take it up with Father Ricardo. Rosie didn't sleep at all that night.

The next day, she was out of bed, dressed and sitting in the cafeteria, trying to recite a prayer she had never heard in her life, by six o'clock in the morning. Discreetly she looked around the crowded cafeteria for her brother, but there were no boys. And she couldn't find Christine, because all the girls looked the same, with the same haircuts, the same clothes and the same solemn expressions.

After breakfast they sat for Bible class, where Rosie learned that only English would be spoken. If any Indian language were even whispered, there was harsh punishment. Since most of the children came from families who spoke their language mainly, harsh punishment was common. Multiple offenders had wooden blocks tied crossways in their mouths for hours, sometimes longer, causing irreparable damage to their jaws.

After Bible class, Sister Bernadette met Rosie in the hallway and told her, with a smile, to report to the main office. Father Ricardo would see her there. The name "Ricardo" sent a chill through Rosie, but the Sister had smiled, so it could be that Christine would be allowed to stay with her. She reported to the woman at the desk and was told to stand in the corner and wait until father Ricardo asked for her. She stood there for more than an hour, without moving or speaking.

When the door finally opened, the priest stuck his head out, pointed at Rosie and indicated for her to come. He was standing at his desk as she walked in, and she noticed that he was still holding the willow stick. The room smelled of pipe tobacco.

"I hear that you are not happy with your sleeping arrangements," he said calmly.

Rosie shook her head. "No sir," Rosie kept her eyes down, "I just think my sister should—"

The priest cut her off, "Take down your pants."

"Pardon me, sir?"

He slapped his desk with the stick, which made a sound like a gunshot.

Rosie pulled her pants down to her ankles.

"Your panties also," he ordered, slapping the stick against the palm of his other hand.

Rosie did as she was told, but her entire body began to shake uncontrollably.

"Now, bend down over my desk and hold on to the other side of the desk."

Again, she did as she was told. Now she was crying.

Suddenly, the priest's willow was smacked soundly against her bare buttocks and she screamed out. Then again, but harder. And one more time, but lower, against the back of her legs. Rosie's pain was greater than she had ever imagined could be possible. She was sliding off Ricardo's desk when he grabbed her by the back of her shirt and forced her to remain face down, pressed against his paperwork. She felt his cold hand on her bottom. His fingers squeezed her skin and probed her. He roughly forced a finger inside her. He whispered closely into her ear, "If you tell anyone what punishment you receive here, your little sister will receive it worse." He jabbed his finger deep enough to break her hymen and she cried out. "Do I make myself understood?"

"Yes, Father!" Rosie cried.

"Good. Now pull up your pants and get to class," the priest said, with disgust.

Things only got worse in the following days and weeks. Rosie was a model student and never spoke out of place. She never behaved less than perfectly. But every week she was called into Father Ricardo's office for "punishment." The priest always started the same way, having her pull down her trousers and panties, spanking her soundly with his stick while he held her head down. But from there, it developed into a variety of attacks that resulted in Rosie being raped in many ways. After a few weeks, Rosie didn't scream and didn't cry. She became totally submissive to Father Ricardo. Nothing that he did could hurt her any further now.

When Rosie finally became pregnant, at the age of fourteen, she certainly had no idea there was a baby developing inside her. Only Father Ricardo was aware of the conception, and he was very aware that it had taken place six weeks before. When her periods stopped coming, he stopped raping her.

When the Sister came and pulled Rosie from her chores in the kitchen and told her to get a small bag packed with a change of clothes and her toiletries, Rosie thought she would be going home. She was positive that

Leonard and Christine would be waiting at the gate for her, with her mommy and daddy.

But it was Father Ricardo who was waiting for her in his car. The Sister opened the back door, Rosie got in with her bag and the door was slammed shut. As the priest pulled away from the school, Rosie turned to look back. She was sure that beyond the rising cloud of dust, she could see her brother clutching the wire fence with one hand and waving to her with the other.

The priest drove all day, stopping only once for gas and junk food to go. Rosie didn't ask where they were going, but she knew for sure that they were travelling away from of her home. By the mileage signs, she could tell that they were getting closer and closer to Vancouver, a city she had only heard of in the stories of her more adventurous uncles.

As they got closer to Vancouver, the traffic became heavier and more chaotic. Rosie's head was spinning with movement and noise. Soon she noticed that they were following the airport signs, and it wasn't long before she saw the huge airliners in the distance. Before that moment, the biggest plane she had ever seen was a Beaver, a float plane that would land on the lake in front of their cabin a couple of times a year.

The priest pulled into the day parking lot and told Rosie to take her bag and follow him. They walked into the terminal, went up an escalator and straight to a line of chairs facing large windows that looked over the runway. Planes were landing and taking off. She saw a man and a woman sitting in two of the chairs, silently staring ahead. The priest sat next to the man and indicated for Rosie to sit next to the woman. They were a nice looking, well-dressed couple, both dark like Indians, and they offered Rosie friendly smiles.

Father Ricardo pulled out an envelope and offered it for the man to see. They spoke during the meeting in a language Rosie couldn't understand. The man accepted the envelope, removed the contents and inspected all the papers carefully. Satisfied, he put the papers back in the envelope and slipped it inside his coat pocket. He pulled another envelope from the other coat pocket and gave it to Father Ricardo, which the priest opened and inspected. Rosie could see that it contained money, a lot of money. The priest shook hands with both the man and the woman and then rose to his feet. Without saying a word to Rosie, he turned and walked away.

When they arrived in Santiago, Chile, Rosie had no idea of where in the world she was or why she was there. She did know that they had flown for many hours in a big plane, far away from the residential school and far away from Father Ricardo. But also far away from Lenny and Christine. She wanted to feel happy but she worried for her brother and sister, and she fretted over whether she would ever see them again.

The couple took her in a taxi straight from the airport to an apartment in the city, where they handed her over to a stout, middle-aged woman and they disappeared. Rosie had not said one word to them the entire trip. In fact, she had been silent since she had left the residential school. And she had not eaten, nor slept. Exhaustion, hunger and loneliness began to crash over her.

The woman sat Rosie down at the kitchen table and put a bowl of lentil soup in front of her. She smiled and Rosie could see that she was missing a tooth and was reminded of her mother's sister, Auntie Sara. The woman also had the same round face and wore her thick, black hair up in a bun like Auntie Sara. As Rosie ate the soup, she gazed around the woman's apartment. She saw religious shrines, assorted rosaries and plastic saints on every shelf. The woman busied herself around the kitchen and talked non-stop in Spanish. Rosie paid no attention until after she had satisfied her hunger. Then she let the woman know with her hands that she didn't speak the language.

The woman stopped and sat across from Rosie. She pointed to Rosie and said, "Rosario Venegas." Then she pointed to herself and said, "Señora."

Rosie shook her head and pointed to herself. "Rosie Frank," she corrected.

The woman shook her head. "No," she said. "Ahora, Rosario Venegas."

"No," Rosie said forcefully.

Señora's expression turned sad. "No," she repeated, and pointed again to Rosie. "Rosario Venegas."

Tears began to roll down Rosie's cheeks. She felt alone and wanted her father. "I am Rosie Frank," she pleaded. "I'm from Long Lake. I have a brother and a sister." She put her arms out in exasperation. "I have a mother and a father!"

Señora came to Rosie's side and held her as she cried. After the sobbing slowed, Señora pointed to Rosie's stomach. "Bebé," she said, and offered a consoling smile.

Rosie's red, tear-stained eyes went wide. "What?"

Señora rubbed Rosie's stomach in a circular motion. "Bebé," she repeated.

Rosie was confused. She knew where babies came from and how they were made, but she never related what the priest did to her with having a baby. What Father Ricardo did was punishment. She was taught that having a baby was a gift. She was stunned speechless.

In the days that followed, Rosie learned, through sign language and simple words, many things that left her even more confused. She listened to the Señora and asked questions as if it was all somebody else's story. Her name had been changed to Rosario Venegas to match the name on the Chilean passport Father Ricardo gave the man and woman at the Vancouver airport, the same couple who had bought the baby Rosie was carrying and who had hired Señora to be the mid-wife. The young optometrist and his wife had tried to have a child for five years, but always unsuccessfully. It was due to God's intervention, Señora said, with her hands in the praying position and eyes turned upward, that the couple found Father Ricardo to help them find a child. From the irresponsible sin of a young girl getting herself pregnant, the priest had created a miracle. Now everyone would be blessed. Rosie was never sure what irresponsible sin she had committed, but now she was convinced that she deserved what was happening to her. It was God's will.

As the baby developed in the following weeks and months, a good working relationship developed between Rosie and Señora. Rosie was a fast learner in Spanish and Señora was very helpful and patient. In fact, as long as Rosie followed Señora's rules, didn't challenge her limits and showed respect, Señora was helpful and patient. Rosie was so happy to be beyond the reach of Father Ricardo that she would do everything exactly as Señora asked and would pray to the Virgin exactly when Señora prayed to the Virgin. Rosie always prayed for her family. Señora prayed for the baby.

By the time the baby was ready to enter the world and make very happy parents of the Chilean couple, Rosie's Spanish was better than her English. And she prayed to the Virgin with as much faith and emotion as Señora herself. She had found a safe place.

———

Leonard and Christine stared ahead, wide-eyed and stunned into silence. They didn't hear Rosie's question. "Have you had enough tea?" she repeated.

They nodded their heads in unison.

"I'll have Sister Catalina bring us some ice water," she said, "and maybe some sandwiches."

Leonard and Christine again nodded together in silence.

Finally Leonard asked, "So I'm an uncle?"

"Well, technically and biologically," Rosie admitted, nonchalantly, "yes, you are an uncle and Christine is an aunt. But I didn't even see the baby. I gave birth in Señora's apartment and the baby was taken away immediately. I never even knew if it was a girl or a boy. The next day, Señora drove me to the airport. On the way, she explained that I was flying to Buenos Aires, where a woman whom Father Ricardo had arranged, would pick me up at the airport. I was to be one of her house-keepers."

"Fucking cold-hearted assholes," Christine muttered.

"Christine," Leonard said, flipping his eyes toward Rosie, "try to watch your language."

She ignored his suggestion. "Jesus, I'd like to cut out his eyeballs with a dull knife."

"Rosie, what happened when you arrived in Buenos Aires?" Leonard asked to divert the conversation away from Christine.

"The woman who picked me up was named María del Carmen. She was a dignified older woman, and very nice to me from the beginning. She was the owner of this estate where we now sit. She lived alone in this mansion because she had been widowed when her husband was tragically murdered in a small restaurant in San Telmo. He was a wealthy businessman and politician in Buenos Aires and, like most people in that class, had close Mafia-type connections. María, a well known actress from Chile, was his trophy wife. She inherited his estate and fortune when he was killed.

"I was sent here to be her laundry girl. There were two other housekeepers already here, girls a couple of years older than me, who I worked with and with whom I shared a room. Late at night when we talked in our beds, I learned a lot from them. Sister Catalina was actually Katy Bob, a Carrier Indian like us, from Prince George. Ricardo had gotten her pregnant when she was just thirteen years old. She went through the same as me, but handed over to another Chilean couple and a different midwife. The oldest housekeeper, Sister Elisa – you'll meet her - was Melinda Henry, from a reserve near Williams Lake in British Columbia. She arrived here a year before Catalina, and went through the same thing. She was fifteen then."

"That bastard Ricardo had a fucking baby mill happening," Christine growled. "I guess he found it more rewarding to sell babies than to save souls"

"Did María del Carmen realize where her flow of housekeepers was coming from?" Leonard asked. "Was she part of Ricardo's organization?"

"Did she know the truth?" Rosie said. "No, she didn't. She was told that we were orphaned Indian girls, with no families and that we all had "inappropriate relations" with many men. She knew about the pregnancies and about the immediate adoptions arranged for needful couples. She was also told that we needed to be saved from lives of destitution and, very likely, prostitution. María del Carmen did not come from a wealthy family, so she understood. She was happy to take us on, one by one, and to give us a stable and nurturing home. She was a very generous woman."

"So," Leonard said thoughtfully, "María del Carmen did not play a conscious role in Ricardo's baby trafficking. Then why were you all sent to the same place by different midwives?"

Rosie paused for a sip of tea. She was having trouble articulating the answer. "María del Carmen took us girls in as a favour to her older brother, Father Ricardo."

Leonard's jaw dropped. He looked around the room, stunned. Then he turned to face his sister. "You mean, this is the home of Ricardo's sister?"

Rosie nodded.

"That man will stop at nothing to take everything," Leonard said. He squeezed his fists until the knuckles turned white. "I think I could actually kill him. Did you ever hear from María where he ended up?"

"Yes," Rosie replied. "I know where he is."

———

Rosario enjoyed her new life at the hacienda of María del Carmen. She lived each day with gratitude and appreciation for the security she felt within the sanctuary of the red brick wall surrounding the estate. She loved her new friends, Catalina and Elisa, as if they were her sisters and María treated them all as more than servants. María had a tutor come in three times a week to teach her girls how to read, write and do simple arithmetic. She herself taught them proper Spanish and etiquette. And Rosie worked and learned with an unflagging determination to please María del Carmen. She wanted to give to María as much as she had received. She wanted María del Carmen to love her, as she loved María del Carmen. Not one of the girls revealed the truth about her past, fearing María would kick her out onto the streets.

Then, after three years, the truth did come out. The day after Rosie turned seventeen, Father Ricardo showed up at the estate. He told her that saving Indian souls in Canada had taken a toll on his spirit and that he needed to rest in another environment. He did not reveal that he had been caught by Sister Bernadette with his finger inside a twelve year old girl and that he had been excommunicated. María del Carmen was surprised and elated to see him, and happy to have him stay with her.

The night Father Ricardo arrived, Rosie and the other girls hid in her bedroom and held each other, consumed with fear. All three had erased everything in the past that had anything to do with the priest. Now the girls would have to face their shameful pasts and worst fears.

At first, Father Ricardo ignored the girls and only acknowledged María, whom he spoke to calmly and respectfully. It was hard to believe he was the same man. Rosie was also surprised by how big and heavy the priest had become. Even his red, pox-marked face was puffed-out smooth. His moustache had turned white, while his thinning hair remained black. Inwardly and outwardly, the priest seemed to be a different person.

He had only been in María's house for a week, when his pious curtain fell.

Rosie was alone in the laundry room folding sheets when he suddenly appeared and closed the door behind him. His expression immediately turned dark and the sadistic grin returned to his face.

"Did you think that I forgot you, Miss Frank?" he said in English. "I could never forget you." He approached her slowly. "You've turned into a very pretty young lady and I know you have sinned." He stopped directly in front of her. "Now you must redeem yourself. Get on your knees," he demanded.

Rosie's body shook with fear. She dropped to her knees and began to cry.

The priest unbuttoned his pants and pressed himself against Rosie's face. "You know what to do. Now do it!" He grabbed her by her hair and tried to force himself into her mouth. At that moment, María del Carmen walked in with a blouse she needed to be ironed. She saw her brother with his pants undone and clutching the back of Rosario's head. Rosario was on her knees and crying.

María flew into a rage. She screamed at her brother. "What are you doing?"

"Get out of here," he ordered her. "I'm teaching this heathen how to repent."

María attacked him with flailing arms and fingernails. The priest tried to fight her off, but she had totally lost her mind and she went at him without fear. All the respect and admiration that she held for her brother had evaporated in a second. "I'll kill you!" she screamed. She scratched his face, kicked his groin and bit his arm. Ricardo responded brutally by attacking his sister like a rabid dog. He slugged her in the face, knocking her to the floor and he began kicking her violently.

Seeing an opportunity, Rosie grabbed one of his legs so that he would stop kicking María. The priest then hit the back of Rosie's head with his closed fist and screamed, "You savage bitch!" He hit her again, harder. "You shall repent!"

Suddenly Ricardo stopped fighting and yelling. His scarlet red face had sweat dripping from the jowls. He looked confused. He clutched his chest and stared vacantly at his sister, groaning and bleeding on the floor. His legs went weak and began to wobble. His huge body weaved. Then his eyes went wide and he toppled over.

—

Leonard and Christine followed Rosie out of the sun room, up another staircase and down a hallway into a darker part of the house.

"Where are you taking us?" Christine asked. "To the torture room? This is almost scary. You should get some lighting up here, hang a few pictures of God, or Jesus, or something, to brighten it up."

Rosie didn't respond. It was as if she had not heard. She led her brother and sister silently to the last door in the hallway, took a key out of her pocket and motioned for them to follow her in.

The room was no lighter than the hallway. A smell of sickness, alcohol and disinfectant permeated the air. As Leonard's eye's adjusted to the darkness, he saw an old man in a bed hooked up with tubes and beeping monitors. He seemed to be dead. His face was twisted and contorted, with pasty white skin stuck on a skull. His eyes were open, but they were milky and unresponsive to his visitors. An old man holding a bed pan appeared from an adjoining room door and nodded to Rosie. He then went about his business, changing the pan and wiping the slobber from the chin of a dying old man. He was gone in less than a minute.

"This is Ricardo?" Leonard asked.

"Yes," Rosie said. "This is the man you want to kill."

"Looks like he's already dead," Christine said.

"He had a severe stroke during the fight with me and María. It left him completely incapacitated. María insisted that Catalina, Elisa and I tell her everything that had happened before, leaving nothing out. Once she heard our stories, she was devastated. She suggested that she arrange for the three of us to stay in a convent so we could be safe and she could deal with her brother and the trauma he brought to her house. So, we all agreed and moved to the convent, and studied to become nuns. She put Ricardo up here, and kept him alive through these tubes and machines. She hired the old man to be his nurse as he deteriorated. She followed our progress at the convent and kept in touch with us. And when we left the convent, she was waiting for us.

"María persuaded us to come back to her estate, to live with her. She said that she had cancer and would die soon, which in fact she did, only two months later. In her will she left everything to us, including the estate and a substantial amount of money. She made only two requests: that her brother never leaves this room alive, and that he is kept alive, as long as possible, with the minimum amount of pain medication. He was beyond help, or improvement, at that time, and now he has prostate cancer. He has suffered in this room for thirty years, and I can't see him lasting much longer."

Leonard walked over to the bedside and looked down at the hateful man who had ruined so many lives. No life emanated from his filmy eyes, and his shrunken body barely made a bump under the bed sheets. But now Leonard felt nothing - not hate, not anger, not compassion, not even redemption. There was nothing he had to say to this mindless, sick old man. The priest was already gone.

Christine stepped up beside Leonard. She took his hand in hers. "I guess we can get a life now."

"Yeah," he replied and took a deep breath, almost a sigh. Then he smiled at his little sister and squeezed her hand. "I could use some air," he said.

Rosie spoke up from the doorway. "I think Sister Catalina was going to bring sandwiches to the outside patio."

They seated themselves around the patio table, and soon Sister Catalina and Sister Elisa joined them for lunch. As they ate sandwiches and drank lemonade, each of them talked about the parts of their childhood they could remember, such as the smell of moose stew simmering and fry bread fresh off the woodstove. Sitting in the outhouse at minus-forty degrees and watching the northern lights dancing across the sky. The excitement of a relative returning to the reserve from town bearing special treats and presents. Picking soapberries to be whipped up with sugar to produce Indian ice cream.

At last, Leonard asked the nuns, "Why don't you come back to Canada now?"

All three of them looked at each other with blank faces.

Rosie spoke for them all. "At first, when María found out the truth, she asked us if we wanted to go back. I think, at that point, maybe we all felt too ashamed, and even responsible for what had happened to us. Also, Canada was not nice to Indian girls, and the convent sounded like the safe haven we needed at the time. Since then, I think we have realized that our central relationship is with God and that our mission is here."

"Well, it's a little better in Canada," Christine said. "It doesn't suck so much now."

Rosie smiled, "Well, I'm proud of both of you. Leonard is an important fire expert and you are a successful newspaper reporter."

"Yeah, I'm a big success," Christine said, with a hint of sarcasm. "And that brings me to a special request I have for you. I do a lot of interviews with elders and other First Nation members with interesting stories to tell. I was thinking that since Leonard has spent all this money to get me here—"

"What money?" Leonard cut her off.

Christine waved him off. "The money you keep hidden in the can," she said, and then continued to address Rosie. "I wouldn't mind hanging around for a few days. I'd like to do interviews with all of you about your experiences. These stories might help a lot of people with their healing.

"I'm not so sure," Rosie replied, looking at Sister Catalina and Sister Elisa for a response. They both shrugged their shoulders. "There are things nuns just don't relive in the newspaper, Christine."

"We can change your name to protect the innocent. You would be helping countless others with their battles from the past. You would be giving hope to the friggin' world of the oppressed."

Rosie laughed, "I think I know why you're a successful journalist."

———

Marcela spent three hours listening to Diego complain about everything from the fit of his shoes to the state of the nation, while all she wanted was to drop off the report and leave. She even had Ernesto wait in the car, because she had intended to be only a few minutes. Of course, Ernesto had no problem killing a few hours, flirting with the girls on the sidewalk and joking with the other waiting drivers. He was ready, however, and did deliver Marcela to the estate fifteen minutes after Leonard had phoned.

"So, how did it go?" Marcela asked as Leonard got in the back seat next to her.

"It was a life-changing experience," he answered.

Christine had slipped in the front seat. "No kidding," she agreed. "It definitely filled a big hole."

"I am happy for you," Marcela said. "You must be exhausted, Christine."

"Yes, I am. I need about twenty-four hours in bed. Ernesto, can you bring me to a hotel?"

"No hay problema, Señora."

"I don't know why you didn't take Rosie's offer of staying with her," Leonard said.

"Because that place creeps me out, with the corpse upstairs and nuns wandering around. I need sleep, not haunting."

"We can take her to the place you were staying, Leonard," Marcela suggested.

"*Were* staying?" Christine asked. "Where are you staying now?" There was an uncomfortable pause, while Leonard and Marcela glanced at each other. "Oh, I get it," she said.

"Maybe I should stay at the hotel," Leonard said to Marcela. Now both Ernesto and Christine rolled their eyes. "I've inconvenienced you enough."

"You're leaving tomorrow," Marcela said. "There's no sense in moving everything for one night."

"Well," Leonard said, "if you don't mind, it would be easier."

Christine looked over at Ernesto. "Is this conversation stupid, or do they think that we don't get it?"

Ernesto grinned. "I'm going with stupid."

"I should warn you about Ernesto," Marcela said to Christine, redirecting the uncomfortable conversation away from herself and Leonard. "He has no morals when it comes to women."

Leonard laughed, "Having no morals is a prerequisite for Christine."

"Listen to them," Christine said to Ernesto. "Like they're vestal virgins. Besides, I hate to tell you, Ernie, but I'm older than you think."

Now it was Marcela's turn to laugh. "That's not going to stop him for a second."

Leonard added, "And, as if he didn't already know that you're twice his age."

"Okay," Christine retorted. "Maybe I'm not that tired."

Ernesto got the point and played along. "Perhaps you would like to experience the night life of Buenos Aires," he grinned. "I could show you a good time."

"Sounds excellent to me. But do you think we can lose the two puritans in the back seat? We don't want to be held back by their strict moral code." She turned and looked back at Leonard. Marcela was holding his hand and he was glowing. "Oh great," Christine said, turning back to Ernesto. "I thought he was going to leave tomorrow, and I'd be free from the glaring eye of my big brother and the real fun could begin."

Leonard's eyes, now seeming much softer and browner, turned to Marcela, who could feel her own euphoria radiating through her eyes and her smile.

"No," Leonard said, more to Marcela than to Christine. "I should be responsible and probably shouldn't leave you here alone."

CHAPTER TWELVE

Day Seven
December 24, 2001

Leonard opened his eyes and looked at the digital clock on the night stand. 6:59. He felt Marcela's warm body spooned into his, he could feel her legs tight to his legs and her breasts against his back. He felt her breathing against the nape of his neck. He closed his eyes and fell asleep again, content that he would be spending Christmas in Argentina.

July 30, 1945
Misión de Nuestra Señora de la Colina
Santiago, Chile

Ricardo stood outside Father Antonio's office, nervously shifting his weight from foot to foot and wiping the sweat from the palm of his hands onto his Altar Server's white cotton surplice. He could not imagine why the priest would order him to be at his office at eight o'clock. He had performed all his duties exactly as he had been shown, because he did not want to disappoint the priest. He had walked with the candle and it had not gone out once. He had thought, after the service, that his family would be so proud of him, especially María. He wanted so much to show his mother, father and his sister that he could become a priest himself.

Ricardo knew that he was a disappointment for his parents. His mother never missed the opportunity to reaffirm that he was ugly, sickly and not as smart as she expected him to be. But María had faith in Ricardo and convinced him that priesthood was his destiny and the best way to gain favour with the two most important treasures in life, God and family.

Ricardo, though not particularly religious, took his sister's word as gospel truth and went to the Misión de Nuestra Señora de la Colina, the preparatory boarding school, with a determination to please God and family and to do whatever it took to become a priest. María always knew what was best for him.

The clock on the wall clicked right on eight o'clock.

Convinced that how he behaved in the following fifteen minutes would determine the rest of his life, thirteen-year-old Ricardo del Carmen wiped the sweat from his hands one more time, gathered his resolve to please and knocked on the door to Father Antonio's office.

AUTHOR'S NOTES

NATIONS APART is a fictional story which is set within factual historic scenarios. While the main characters and their particular situations are products of my imagination, most of the events and some of the names are real. To the extent that real persons and reported events are mentioned in the novel, I have included such references without the knowledge or cooperation of the individuals involved. Other than the names mentioned below and well-known individuals and news events referred to for purposes incidental to the plot, all names, places, characters and events are straight from my imagination, and any resemblance to actual events, locales, or persons, living or dead, is entirely coincidental.

All of the words written here have been put down with my deep and sincere respect for all the abused of the Canadian residential schools, the victims on both sides of the Dirty Wars in Argentina and every soldier that died on Las Islas Malvinas/the Falkland Islands.

It's important to note; while the Long Lake Indian Reserve and the Mary Lake Residential School are fictional locations, the horrific abuses described were factual in many residential schools. This novel barely scratches the surface.

The escape from the Rawson prison was a real event and I took the liberty of using a few actual names: union spokesperson Augusto Tosco, the coerced guard Fazio and the Montonero leader Fernando. The prison guard who was shot and killed during the actual escape was Juan

Antonio Valenzuela. Their roles in this novel have been dramatized to suit the story.

The battle at Mount Longdon went down pretty much as I describe. Lieutenant Ramos and Second Lieutenant Baldini were actual Argentine heroes in a war waged from both sides for purely selfish political reasons. These men should be remembered for their bravery and dedication to their fellow soldiers.

In memory…

Carlos Alberto Astudillo
Alfredo Elías Kohon
María Angélica Sabelli
Rubén Pedro Bonet
Eduardo Adolfo Capello
Mario Emilio Delfino
Alberto Carlos del Rey
Clarisa Rosa Lea Place
José Ricardo Mena
Miguel Ángel Polti
Ana María Villareal de Santucho
Humberto Segundo Suarez
Humberto Adrián Toschi
Jorge Alejandro Ulla
Susana Graciela Lesgart de Yofre
Maríano Pujadas
Alberto Miguel Campos
María Antonia Berger
Ricardo René Haidar
and
Juan AntonioValenzuela

ABOUT THE AUTHOR

The author is a retired firefighter, gold miner, teacher, surveyor, log builder, innkeeper, self-publisher, bartender and writer. He and his wife spend their time between homes in northern British Columbia and the southern Andes of Argentina.